REUNITED LOVERS

FRIENDSHIP CHRONICLES 2

SHELLEY MUNRO

MUNRO PRESS

Reunited Lovers

Print ISBN: 978-1-99-106331-1
Digital ISBN: 978-0-9941483-7-7

Editor: Evil Eye Editing

Cover: Kim Killion, The Killion Group, Inc.

Munro Press, New Zealand.

First Munro Press electronic publication July 2017

First Munro Press print publication June 2023

DEDICATION

For Paul, my partner in crime and fellow adventurer.

"Because in the end, you won't remember the times you spent in the office or mowing your lawn.
Climb that goddamn mountain." – Jack Kerouac

Introduction

Julia Maxwell is a seize-the-moment party girl until the night she spends with up-and-coming rocker Ryan Callander. From that moment, she becomes a one-man woman. Pity he hasn't kept with the program.

Tired of the secrets that have kept her out of the press and Ryan's fans happy, angry with mounting evidence of infidelity, Julia is older, wiser, and determined to divorce his cheatin' ass.

Ryan's long European tour had more than its share of hard knocks—one of which landed on his head when he was mugged. Divorce papers waiting for him at home are a shock that fills in some of the holes in his sketchy memory. But it could be too late to salvage his marriage.

If Ryan thinks flirtatious smiles, seductive touches, and hot-and-heavy kisses are going to smooth things over, Julia's got a hammer with his name on it. To her surprise, he calls her bluff, determined to rebuild a bright future for both of them. But the past is lurking with some missing pieces that could bring their hearts crashing down.

Warning: Contains a pissed ex-stripper turned burlesque dancer, a bunch of nosy friends and a smooth-talking rocker with one thing on his mind. Stripper poles and skimpy costumes are optional.

CHAPTER ONE

"Fuck!" Ryan Callander stared at the paper in his hand, shock ratcheting up the low-grade headache he'd had for the last two hours. Julia wanted a divorce. He concentrated on breathing—in, out, in, out—to stem his escalating panic.

Caleb popped his tousled dark head from a bedroom of the inner-city Auckland apartment they'd shared for the past five years. "What is it, man?" He glanced at Ryan and grimaced at the envelope. "Can't the mail wait until we've had some sleep? This jetlag is kicking my butt."

God, she couldn't do this. It was a misunderstanding. She'd realize once he explained everything. "No, I have to go out."

Caleb cursed and disappeared. He reappeared with a black T-shirt in his hands and yanked it over his head. "I'm coming with you."

"I don't need a babysitter," Ryan snapped.

"Your memory is still spotty. What kind of friend would let you loose in the big bad city alone?"

Ryan made a scoffing sound. "It's Auckland. I remembered the location of our apartment. I can call a cab."

"But you didn't recall where the mystery woman lives—the one you kept muttering about in hospital."

"I'm going to her now." He'd recalled more about Julia than he'd let on to Caleb, their manager and the rest of the band. The only thing he couldn't remember was how to contact her—that and her last name. Caleb had told Ryan he didn't have a serious woman in New Zealand, not one he cared about. Ryan knew different, but the harder he'd tried to remember the more his head had ached.

"And if your mystery woman is a groupie?" Caleb asked, his expression making his opinion clear. *French Letters'* groupies didn't warrant midnight visits from the band. "Surely it can wait until we've at least caught a few hours of sleep. Besides, Seymour will have a hernia if you out yourself to a groupie. You can't visit one without full makeup or a mask. Remember the terms of our contract."

"You can sleep," Ryan said. "I'm going out now." He picked up his wallet and phone, both new since the police never recovered the ones stolen from him while the band had been playing in Europe.

"Wait, damn it." Frustration shimmered in his friend's

voice, but Ryan didn't slow. Running thumps echoed down the hall. "Fuck, Ryan. I'm coming with you. Give me a chance to put on my boots."

Ryan slowed. "I'll hail a cab. If you're not outside in five minutes, I'm going without you." A mixture of anxiety and anger pumped through his veins. Julia wasn't any damn groupie. She'd already seen him without his makeup. His mouth curled to a grin as fragments of memories pushed past the fog in his mind. She'd seen him in a lot less and loved the view.

He checked the street and spied a cab. Hell, luck was with him. It was a sign. He waved, elated when the taxi halted beside him, and spoke to the driver, reading the address off the formal document before jumping into the back of the cab. He glanced back for his friend.

Caleb appeared in the doorway, glimpsed the cab and cursed a blue streak. He increased his pace to a sprint. Breathless, he flung himself into the back seat with Ryan. "I fuckin' told you to wait."

"I intended to wait."

"Didn't bloody look like it. Where are we going anyway?"

"Parnell."

"Give me more. Who are we going to see?"

"Julia." Ryan fell silent, waiting to see if Caleb remembered her.

"Wait, Julia? Not that blonde bird we both banged last

summer?" Caleb's smirk was a toothy one. It made Ryan itch to thump him.

"Watch your mouth." Ryan concentrated on his clenched fists instead of the urge to beat up his friend. Caleb didn't understand. If he realized, he wouldn't talk that way. When Caleb opened his mouth to say something else, Ryan cut him off. "Watch what you say about Julia or I'll tell your mother on you."

"What are we? Five years old?" Caleb stared at him in astonishment. "You sound like my sister."

A sharp pain sliced through his head, and he rubbed it with his fingers.

Caleb's eyes narrowed. "Is your head hurting again?"

"Yeah." His anxiety made it throb worse than normal. The doctors said his headaches would tail off after a while. He wished he knew when that would be, 'cause it had been months.

"I'll help you as much as I can."

"Yeah, I know." He and Caleb had been best friends since they were five. It was weird how he recollected everything about Caleb and growing up together. He even remembered the words to their songs, yet his time with Julia remained blank. Those precious snippets of memories had taken weeks to return to him after the mugging, and even now his mind contained frustrating gaps.

The cab slowed and came to a halt outside a new

apartment block. He didn't recognize it, but he and the rest of the band had been in Europe for almost a year, much longer than they'd originally planned. Now that he was here, nerves slid through him. His heart beat a little faster. He paid the driver, grimacing at the faint tremor in his hand.

Caleb watched the taxi drive off. "Are we going to be here a while?"

"Depends." Ryan strode to the apartment entrance and checked the directory on the wall. Julia Maxwell. Only her Christian name seemed familiar while the surname could belong to anyone. He pressed on her apartment buzzer, keeping his finger down for long seconds. He waited. When nothing happened, he stabbed the button again.

"She's either a deep sleeper or she's not home. Maybe she's out on a date."

Ryan's gut twisted, a sharp pain of protest. "No," he whispered, appalled at the idea.

Caleb's dark brows rose. "Just because you've given up dating and become a monk, it doesn't mean the rest of the world should follow your example. What's so important about Julia?"

Ryan sighed. He pushed the bell one final time, and when nothing happened, turned to his friend, his shoulders slumping in defeat.

"Ryan, I don't get it. Why is it so urgent for you to see this Julia?"

Ryan's chest ached in tandem with the throb at his temples. "Julia is my wife."

"What?" Caleb grabbed his arm, pincher fingers digging into his biceps. "Why didn't you say something?"

"The time never seemed right. My memory was patchy, so there was nothing to tell."

"Fuck, she must have been worried sick when she didn't hear from you. Why didn't she ring?"

"She probably tried," Ryan said. "They took my phone. Even if she managed to get in touch with Seymour, he wouldn't have believed her. And because the mugging happened between concerts and we only had to cancel one, she most likely thinks I abandoned her."

"You should have told me, man."

Ryan tried not to let the pain inside him gain momentum. "At first I couldn't remember her name. Everything was so foggy I decided my memory might play tricks on me. Besides, Seymour would have had a cow."

"The 'no serious relationships' thing? There's no reason we can't get married if we want."

Ryan snorted. "That's not what management says. You've heard Seymour's lectures."

"Doesn't mean we have to follow his advice," Caleb said. "It's not a formal clause in our contract."

"Is that your year of law talking?"

"Fuck you," Caleb said, giving him a one finger salute for emphasis. "I was humoring my parents. When did you get married anyhow? How did you do it without me noticing?"

"You attended your family christening over Anniversary weekend. Julia and I flew to Fiji for a four-day break and married while we were there."

"Congratulations."

"She's served divorce papers on me," Ryan said with a snarl, anger warring with the jagged knife slicing into his brain. He loved her, damn it. "I'm not letting her go without a fight."

Caleb's grin lit up his face. "And I worried a three-month break might bore me." He rubbed his hands together. "This should be fun."

"There's nothing funny about a divorce."

The amusement quit Caleb. "I know that, man, but I understand you. Julia won't stand a chance. She'll be putty in your hands again in days. I'll be your wingman."

Ryan's hackles rose and his fingers balled to fists. "You won't be putting your hands on my wife again. That was a one-time thing."

Caleb raised his hands in surrender, his gaze steady, reassuring, and some of the tension seeped from Ryan. Caleb was his friend, not the enemy.

"Why don't we go back to the apartment, grab a few hours sleep then stake out her place? You can confront her when we run her to ground."

It was a sensible solution, despite his need for immediate

action. He hesitated before admitting to his exhaustion. The damn headache had taken hold, and his skull thumped like the crazy beat of Neil's drums during a solo spot. "Yeah, okay. Sounds like a plan."

Down but not out. Julia was his wife. His woman, and soon no one would doubt it, least of all her.

She had to get away.

Now, before she bawled. Julia bent to grab her purse, her fingers brushing the envelope containing her mother's letter. Unshed tears—divorce-induced tears—stung her eyes, and she blinked.

"Anyone for another drink?" Julia sprang to her feet, smiling brightly at her three friends while waiting for their reply.

"I'll take another margarita," Maggie said, her brown eyes sparkling with happiness, even in the dim light of the *Cock and Bull* pub.

"I shouldn't," Susan chimed in then wrinkled her pert, freckled nose. "Oh, what the heck. Me too."

Christina waggled her empty glass, setting her golden bracelets chattering in a musical tone. "Same again for me, thanks."

Julia pushed her way through the crowd, scowling at the two suit-wearing buffoons who leered at her boobs.

If anything, her repulsion egged them on, their smirks widening with the thrill of the chase.

"Wanna drink, babe?" Mr. Beard asked, waggling his brows in a suggestive manner.

"Blondes with pretty..." Mr. Shaved Head looked her up and down, his gaze lingering on her breasts. "...eyes are my favorite. Let's cut to the chase and go to my place."

"I'm taken," she snapped, stomping past. Her loneliness, her rotten taste in men, swirled amongst her concern for her mother. Her soon-to-be divorce. A tear plopped onto her arm. Another struck the hem of her lacy white top. Instead of forcing her way to the bar, she kept walking until she made the relative privacy of the restrooms. By the time the door whooshed shut behind her, tears were falling in earnest.

Everything was such a mess...

The door pushed open, and Maggie spied her before she could wipe her eyes. Her friend's happy expression faded. "Julia, are you all right?"

Julia swallowed. "Yes."

"Liar, you've been quiet all evening. Come on." She plucked a packet of tissues out of her handbag and handed several over. "Dry your eyes and we'll get out of here. Let's collect Christina and Susan and head to my place. Perhaps we can help."

One taxi ride later, Julia found herself at Connor and Maggie's apartment in Newmarket, not far from the business center of Auckland. Maggie, who had secretly snared Julia's best friend, Connor, last year, bustled around organizing drinks, and soon they each sipped a glass of white wine. A bowl of crisps, another of vegetable sticks and a fattening cheesy dip sat on the glass-topped coffee table in front of them.

"When's Connor due home?" Julia asked—casually, she thought. Judging by the rolling eyes, her friends were on to her plan.

"Quit stalling." Susan confirmed her fears.

Julia ruminated on her secrets—the things she hadn't confided to her friends. Some of them about Ryan she couldn't tell because she'd promised, and she never went back on her word, even if the louse didn't deserve her loyalty.

"Julia, it can't be that bad," Maggie said.

"It's worse." Julia pulled the envelope from her handbag, going for diversion from the most troubling truth. "This is a letter from my mother."

"You never talk about her," Susan said. "Where does she live?"

"Auckland." They lived in the same city, and her mother posted her a letter rather than pick up the phone or email. It said a lot about their relationship.

"But you never... Do you see her?" Maggie asked.

"We talk on the phone, and I drop in to see her once or twice a month." Julia winced. "That sounds heartless, as if

I don't care, but we've never been super close. She's always been busy working or involved with a man." Usually a different one every month, but she didn't voice the thought. It seemed disloyal when her record was no better.

Maggie wrinkled her nose. "I'd be the last one to cast stones. My relationship with my parents isn't worth shouting about. I'm closer to Connor's parents than mine."

"What's the problem?" Susan's blue eyes held genuine concern. "What can we do to help?"

Julia's hand tightened around her glass. Afraid of breaking it, she set her wine aside. How would her friends react? "My mother runs a club on Karangahape Road. A strip club." Julia sucked in a quick breath and scanned her friends' faces, ready for their responses. She'd heard every variation while growing up and had a smartass cut down for each dirty, snide comment.

"K' Road? Really?" The pitch of Maggie's voice rose, clear amusement in the quirk of her lips.

"Is that all you're gonna say?" Julia demanded.

"Why didn't you tell us?" Susan asked.

"My question exactly," Christina said. "It's not a brothel, is it?"

"No!" Julia leapt to her feet, indignation fueling her temper. "It's a strip club. Buck's nights and that sort of thing. I earned enough money stripping to pay for my education rather than taking out student loans."

Silence fell. Susan's mouth dropped open fishlike. Intrigue and silent questions radiated off Christina while Maggie raised her quirk to a smartass grin.

"Any more comments?" Julia asked.

"Well, you trump mine and Connor's kinky spanking by a country mile," Maggie said. "Why didn't you tell us?"

"If you had any idea how people treated me while growing up—the teasing and disgusting remarks—you wouldn't ask that question."

"Actually, I do understand." Maggie reached over to squeeze Julia's hand, her manner serious and more importantly, not passing sentence. "My mother and her scandalous private life made my teenage years hell."

"We're not judging you." Susan tilted her head to the side until she resembled an inquisitive bird. "I'm more intrigued than anything. What's the problem?"

"Has the economy downturn hurt your mother's business?" Christina asked.

Julia winced at the sharp hit of guilt. "My mother is struggling to keep ahead of the bank loans, but she needs to an operation. Her heart isn't good."

"And?" Maggie prompted. "How can we help?"

"Mum hired a manager to cover for her, and yesterday he ran off with the week's takings. The next loan payment is due, and if she can't pay, the bank is threatening to call in her loan. She'll lose everything."

Susan's brows drew together. "Did she go to the police?"

"Yes, but she said they treated her as a nuisance."

Her friends fell silent, leaving Julia to her thoughts. She had the money Ryan had given her and intended to throw it back in his face at the first opportunity, once the divorce became final, but this way was better. She'd write her mother a check and tell her it was from her savings to stall awkward questions.

"What time does your mother's club close?" Christina asked.

"Around four in the morning, earlier if there are no customers. Why?"

Christina's eyes gleamed behind her glasses. "We should visit. It's a perfect assignment for the Tight Five." She referred to their group, the name taken from a rugby term where five players bound in a tight formation to face the opposition team. They were like that. Four women and one man—friends—who used to work together at the accountancy firm and who maintained the friendship away from the job.

"A strip club?" Doubt skittered over Susan's freckled face. "Oh no, I couldn't."

"I think it's a great idea," Maggie said. "Christina's right. This is a Tight Five situation. Well, four anyway since Connor isn't here."

"Why?" Julia scanned her friends, studying their expressions. Christina continued to look mischievous. Clear excitement had Maggie beaming in a toothy manner while Susan's brow knit with plain horror.

Christina made a *tsking* sound at the back of her throat as if it should be obvious. "So we can come up with an action plan to help your mother, of course."

"Before Connor gets back," Maggie reminded them, jumping to her feet. "I'll order a cab." She rifled through the contents of her handbag. "Bother, where is my stupid phone?"

"You want to give Connor a reason to spank you," Julia said.

"He's perfectly able to come up with reasons by himself," Maggie said cheerfully. "I don't have a single problem with our sex life."

"Please keep your satisfaction muted," Christina said in disgust, although naughtiness remained in her eyes. "Some of us don't have a sex life."

"Yeah," Susan said, taking a quick sip of her wine.

"Is there an echo in the room?" Maggie taunted.

"Hell, yeah," Christina said. "We're both plain jealous."

Susan gave an emphatic nod. "Damn straight we are."

Julia picked up a carrot stick and crunched down, not bothering to voice her opinion. A sex life was more trouble than anything. Every time sex entered her mind, she thought of Ryan, and she didn't need a reminder of the rat, thank-you-very-much. The last failure in a lengthy line of sexy bad boys—man could she pick 'em.

"Julia?" Christina waved her hands to get her attention.

Julia's head jerked and she blinked. "What?"

Maggie stabbed her cell phone with her forefinger. "The cab will be here in ten minutes. Drink lively, ladies."

Julia found herself swept from Maggie's apartment in a determined storm of friends. They piled into the cab, tipsy from margaritas and wine.

"Give the driver the address, Julia," Christina said.

"Are we sure this is a clever idea?" Susan asked.

"Think of it this way, Susan," Maggie said. "When you're at the *Farmer Seeks a Wife* interviews, you'll have something novel to discuss with your farmer."

"I won't get past the first round," Susan said.

"Then I'm gonna beat your ass," Christina announced, almost crowing. "Because I intend to go all the way, baby. I'm gonna score me a sexy-hot farmer husband."

Susan opened and closed her mouth. "Dang, I'm slipping. I'm doing that negative, judgmental thing again." She took a deep breath. "This will be a fun adventure. Does anyone have a notebook? I can take notes so we don't forget anything."

"How long since you stripped, Julia?" Maggie asked from the front seat.

"Not since I finished my secretarial courses." She glared at the driver when his gaze met hers in the rearview mirror. "I didn't need to work for my mother once I graduated and found a job."

And she couldn't wait to get away from the

score of *uncles* who paraded through her mother's bedroom. The touchy-feely ones had scared her, but she was uncomfortably aware she'd inherited her mother's appalling lack of judgment with men. Now it seemed her mother might move on to women.

Welcome to my crazy world.

Maggie twisted in the front seat to see her friends clearly. "Can you show me a routine or two? Connor would enjoy a private strip show."

"You're talking about sex again," Christina accused.

Maggie giggled, and Julia's heart twisted, a jagged sensation, almost like a sharp blow to the chest. It left her breathless, aching and so alone. While she was pleased for Maggie and Connor, it was painful to see their happiness when she and Ryan... She shook herself, cutting off the thought. Not. Going. There.

Thankfully, the cab pulled up in front of her mother's club. Maggie took care of the fare while the rest of the group climbed out.

"Whoa." Susan gaped at two women in full war paint. With exaggerated hip-swagger, they strutted past in their skimpy skirts and matching tops, their heels *tap-tapping* on the footpath. "I need to work on an attitude like that."

Familiarity seized Julia, the sense of coming home, even though she'd hated living here. The faint throb of a rock ballad seeped through the windows of a flat above a shop farther down the street. Her gaze took in the laughing people waiting for entrance to the new club—another one in opposition to her mother's. The line snaked along the edge of the building and halfway down the next block.

"Watch out," Maggie said, flinging out her arm to stop Julia's progress.

Julia looked down and grimaced. Someone had lost their dinner. She stepped around the smelly pile of vomit. "Do you still want to do this?"

Susan linked her arm with Julia's and grinned. It was a trifle ragged on the edges, but it qualified as a grin. "Yes. Maggie and Christina aren't going to change their minds. I need an adventure to jerk me out of my rut, so you're stuck with us on this mission."

Julia hoped her friends didn't regret their enthusiasm. She steeled herself and headed for the front door of her mother's club—*The Last Frontier*. Not a single person jostled for entry.

"Ladies." An aging security guard stood to attention when he saw them. His white shirt strained over his belly, but he looked sharp with crisply pressed black trousers and black shoes that glistened even in the sparse foyer lighting.

"Hi, Stan," Julia said. "How are you? How are the kids?"

Stan peered at her for an instant and broke into a delighted grin. "Julia, I didn't recognize you. You're so grown up now. Long time no see." He wrapped her in a tight embrace. The scents of tobacco, laundry powder and a hint of Old Spice wafted to her and brought a second flash from the past. Aware of another bout of tears threatening, she pulled away. "Stan, these are my friends Maggie, Christina and Susan. Stan used to supervise me after school when Mum was busy with the club. He made sure I did my homework and was strict about it too. I never got away with anything."

"Not true," Stan said with a fond grin. "She used to wind me around her little finger."

"Ah," Christina said. "So that's your fault. She's still managing the males around her."

Julia turned away, swallowing the lump constricting her throat. Ryan had burrowed into her heart like a parasitic worm, and she hadn't managed him. Not a bit. She forced a smile to her lips, aiming for one that declared she was a competent adult and in complete control. "How's Mum?"

Stan shook his head, his dark brows drawing together. "Not so good. All the stress isn't good for her heart. If I ever see that rat manager I'll wring his neck. Bloody thief, if you'll pardon my French."

"We've come to help," Susan said.

"Good. Elise needs help, no matter how much she refutes it," Stan said. "Go right in, ladies."

"Is it busy tonight?" Julia asked.

A gusty sigh escaped him. "Business is bad this year. The new club down the street has stolen most of our customers. They seem to have a line outside for most of the night."

Christina nudged Maggie. "We'll check out the competition too."

Julia shook her head a fraction, although she didn't attempt verbal dissent. Once an idea wriggled into their heads, her friends became an unstoppable force. Tight Five, indeed.

"How is tomorrow night for you? Since it's Friday, Connor will come with us," Maggie said. "He's playing rugby on Saturday afternoon and won't be drinking. He can be our designated driver."

"It sounds as if our adventure will be a big one," Susan murmured to Julia.

"Yeah." Julia wasn't sure whether to strangle or hug her friends. "I hope you have a thick notepad." She pushed through the internal double doors leading into the club.

The smoke she recalled from her younger years was a thing of the past due to the anti-smoking laws. Instead, a cocktail of alcohol, body odor and strong aftershave greeted her. Her nose wrinkled at the stale atmosphere, and imaginary cooties jumped onto her arms and legs, slithering along her flesh.

"Susan," she said crisply. "Make a note. We need to do something with the air conditioning." They were here now, and she might as well act on her friends' suggestion. Put together an action plan. Even if her mother sold, she'd need to do a few improvements to attract a buyer.

"It's very...ah...interesting," Maggie said, after a quick

glance around the cavernous interior.

"Don't bother with tact," Julia said, taking in the tired décor and carpet stained by numerous drunk and clumsy customers. "It's even worse than I remember."

The red velvet furnishings bore patches, the repairs even more noticeable because of the lack of customers. Up on the stage a young woman with long, chemical-blonde hair and a bored expression went through a lackluster routine. Her jaw worked a piece of gum. That, at least, matched the beat of the music. The song trailed off, and the woman stalked off the stage. Not one man attempted to give her a tip. Not surprising given her second-rate performance.

"We have our work cut out for us," Christina said in woeful understatement.

Nodding, Julia continued to catalog the problems. They needed to gut the entire building and start again. Hire new strippers. Advertise. Get proactive instead of settling for the same old methods, which weren't working. She frowned. Her mother had a knack for the business and could instinctively tell if a woman had what it took to make a good stripper. For the club to go so far downhill and her not realize... Guilt rose to the surface again. She was a bad daughter. She should've checked on her mother more often.

At her side, Susan faltered when a drunken man blundered past on the way to the restrooms. "I'm up for the challenge," she said, her blue eyes bulging as she took in her surroundings.

Maggie swung around in a slow circle, studying every gaping deficiency. She turned to face them and broke into a grin. "Let's do it."

Damn, Julia wanted to weep again. She peered through shimmering eyes at her friends. "The margaritas have rotted your brains."

"I agree with Maggie," Christina said.

Julia glanced at Susan, the normal naysayer and voice of reason. "Are you sure?"

Susan nodded emphatically. "I want to do this."

"I still think you need your heads read by a professional, but let's find my mother. She might talk sense into you." Julia strode up to the bar with her friends at her back. Gratitude she couldn't express clamped around her ribs, making it difficult to breathe. They were the best, but they had no idea what was involved in running a strip club.

A buxom barmaid sauntered up to them as she gulped down the handful of crisps she'd shoved in her mouth. "Yeah, what will it be?"

"Where's Elise?" Julia asked. The woman needed to lose the food habit and her attitude.

"She's out the back." The woman indicated a door behind the bar with a jerk of her finger. "Wait, you can't come back here."

"I'm Elise's daughter," Julia said. "Stan will vouch for me." She stalked to the door, aware of the others hurrying after her.

"Julia?"

Julia paused, shocked by her mother's weak voice. She entered the office and found her mother resting on a couch. She'd lost weight and her blusher stood out in two red circles against the paleness of her cheeks. Her long blonde hair framed her face with lank strands and the distinct gray streaks snared Julia's attention. Her mother was vain when it came to her hair and in the past had ruthlessly dealt with any hint of gray.

"Mum, how are you?"

"I'm fine."

"You're not fine or you wouldn't be in here resting. Why didn't you ring me?" Julia unleashed her worry with sharp words.

Her mother's chin lifted. "I sent you a letter."

"Mum, I live ten minutes away."

"I wanted to tell you everything, and a letter was easier. I didn't want to watch your expression or hear you judge me."

"Oh, Mum." All her childhood embarrassment and their past arguments receded, now unimportant. Her friends were right. They needed a plan, and it might be the thing to take her mind off Ryan. As soon as the divorce came through, she could move on, and meantime, she'd work on helping her mother. "Don't worry about hiring a new manager, not when I can do the job for you."

"I can't ask you to give up your job. You have your own life."

"I'll take a leave of absence," Julia said in a no-nonsense voice, ignoring the tiny sliver of panic struggling to slip free. Her entire life was spinning in the wrong damn direction. "Leave everything to me and you concentrate on getting better."

CHAPTER TWO

RYAN ARRIVED AT JULIA'S apartment the next morning much later than he'd planned. On returning home the previous night, both he and Caleb had crashed, lack of sleep catching up with them. He rang the bell, but as he'd expected, there was no reply. Finally, he returned to their apartment to find an agitated Caleb.

"Where have you been?"

"I went back to Julia's apartment. Either she didn't return home or she'd already left for work." Hell, he hoped it wasn't the first alternative. The idea of Julia in another man's bed kicked like a cranky mule. His hands itched with the need to hit something. Someone. "I'm not an invalid. I made it there and back without getting lost."

Caleb scratched a hand through his scruffy black hair. "I was worried."

"The doctors in Germany said I was fine. Most of my

memories have come back. Hell, if I can remember the words to our songs there's nothing wrong with me."

No matter how much he denied it, Caleb was babying him and smothering him in the process. Ryan knew his friend worried, but he was good, or he would be as soon as he connected with Julia again. "When are you going to Tauranga?"

"Tomorrow."

"And you're staying a week?"

"Yeah, Jeff and Neil have gone home to Wellington. They rang while you were out. They'll be back the week after next so we can knuckle down and sort out new songs for the album."

Ryan absorbed the info and nodded. That gave him a week to do his own thing up here in Auckland. "I might get stuck into the songwriting."

"And Julia?" Caleb passed him a coffee.

Ryan cradled the mug in his hands. "When I catch up to her I'll talk, tell her what happened and ask her to drop the divorce proceedings." He half-expected Caleb to jeer at him, to inform him he was a fool.

"Chicks on tap get old after a while."

Caleb's comment surprised him into a beat of silence. "Neil and Jeff won't agree with you."

"Think how much worse it'd be if the public discovered we were *French Letters*."

"True." Ryan sipped his coffee. "It's great walking down

the street without anyone recognizing me."

"Yeah, there's a lot to be said for mystique and stage makeup," Caleb agreed. "Do you have any ideas for songs?"

"I have half a dozen done already." Ryan couldn't help the spurt of smugness that crept into his tone.

"When? Wait, they'd better not be friggin' soppy ballads."

Ryan shrugged, knowing it would annoy his friend.

Caleb let out a pained groan and clapped a hand to his head. "No! Say it isn't so."

"One or two."

"But you've written rock songs?" A plea.

"Of course." They were some of his best work, but the ballads, inspired by Julia, his mystery woman, were beyond brilliant, even if he said so himself.

"Go get them. You'll have to wait until your girl finishes work before you can see her, anyway. We might as well make use of the hours and get a jump on the arrangements."

At four thirty, Ryan stood and stretched his hands above his head. He groaned, his muscles protesting after sitting for so long. "Time to catch up with my wife."

"I'll give you a lift. I intended to take my car out of mothballs and give it a run anyway."

"You'll leave as soon as she arrives? Give us privacy."

Caleb inclined his head, grabbing his keys as if Ryan had

already agreed with him. "Come on."

They pulled up outside the apartment just as a group of women piled into a cab. "Isn't that Julia?"

Ryan's eyes feasted on his shapely blonde wife, pictured her sparkling brown eyes and sultry smile. "Yeah, follow that cab. I'm not waiting around here all night again." His heart gave several hard thumps before resuming its normal beat.

Caleb shot him a sideward glance. "You can't accost her in public either."

"I'll give her my phone number and ask her to meet me tomorrow for lunch so we can discuss things." Or he'd drag her to bed and keep her locked in his bedroom until she changed her mind about the divorce.

Skepticism bloomed on his friend's face, and Ryan's frustration boiled over. "Don't look at me like that. You foisted yourself on me." He sucked in a quick breath, then let it ease out slow. "Sorry."

"They're heading downtown. Maybe they're going for drinks at one of The Viaduct bars. I hope not. Parking is a bitch around there."

"No problem. You can let me out and go home."

Caleb didn't reply, concentrating on driving instead. "Hell, they're not going to The Viaduct."

They drove up Nelson Street and ended up near Karangahape Road, known locally as K' Road. Ryan stared at the buildings they passed with increasing puzzlement. The street had a sleazy reputation since many of the strip clubs and adult stores were located in the area.

"They're getting out here," Caleb said.

"Why?" Ryan watched Julia plus two other women exit the cab. His hungry gaze roamed her body. She made her black trousers and plain white shirt look sexy.

His.

No matter what she said, they had to give their marriage a chance.

Another cab pulled up in front of the first, and the passengers—a man and woman—joined Julia and her friends. They spoke briefly and entered the black door of a nondescript building. A neon sign flickered, several of the letters not working. *The Last Frontier*, he made out after concentrating on the blinking light.

"Why do they have keys for a strip club?" Caleb asked. "Damn, there's no parking. Wait! No, I see one. The white Nissan is pulling out."

"I have no idea why they're here." Ryan tapped his fingers on his knee while Caleb pulled into the parking space. As soon as the car came to a halt, he clicked his seatbelt free and opened the door. "Let's go."

Julia had disappeared inside. With ground-eating steps, Ryan was at the door in seconds. He tested the handle. Locked. He pounded on the solid surface.

"Hell, Ryan," Caleb said. "If you keep that up, you'll put your fist through it."

The door flew open without warning and he came face-to-face with the guy he'd seen earlier. The man was big, a few inches taller than him, and built solid like a rugby player.

"Who are you?" Ryan demanded.

"We're not open," the man said.

"I want to see Julia."

The man's brows rose. "Who are you?" He tossed Ryan's question back at him.

Ryan shot him a glare, counseling himself to patience when he really wanted to shove the man out of the way. "Ryan Callander. Julia's husband. I'm here to see my wife."

CHAPTER THREE

"ARE WE IN AGREEMENT?" Julia asked after running through the list she'd made during the day.

"Brilliant," Susan said with a trace of awe. "I love the idea of branching out into classes and doing hen's nights is a stroke of genius."

Christina nodded. "Are you sure the burlesque will work? Are there other places that do it or are they strictly strip clubs along K' Road?"

"I did a bit of quick research online. There are no places offering burlesque performances in the area, but it's big overseas. Burlesque might widen our appeal and get more women in the place," Julia said. "What's taking Connor so long?" She took two steps toward the door and came to an abrupt halt. Her pulse roared in her ears like a thundering train, shock threatening to buckle her knees. She staggered two steps before reinforcing her shaking limbs enough to bear her weight.

"Ryan?" she croaked.

"Julia!" Ryan crossed the room and grabbed her into a tight embrace before she could react. His familiar scent rolled over her, masculine with a hint of spicy green and the outdoors. He pressed her head to his chest, apparently content to hold her against his trembling frame. For long seconds she let him, too stunned to react. Then her shock gave way to fury, and she lashed out with her foot, kicking him in the shin.

"Ow!" He released her abruptly, an aggrieved scowl distorting his pretty face. "What did you do that for?"

Cripes, she'd broken her foot, not that she'd admit it to him. She gathered the pain and hurled it back in harsh words. "You can't come waltzing back and expect me to welcome you. Didn't you receive the divorce papers?"

"I don't want a divorce." His blue eyes bored into her. Determined. Steady. He glanced at their avid audience. "We should take this somewhere private."

Julia dug in her heels, feeling contrary. He had no right to burst into her life again. And as for orders—forget it. She squared her shoulders and glowered at him. "They're my friends. They can hear anything you have to say." *Aw, heck. Ryan.* She'd thought she'd hate him... *No!* She hated him. "You cheated on me."

"When did Julia get married?" Susan asked.

Curiosity buffeted Julia in waves, coming at her from all

directions. *Great. Just great.*

She lowered her voice, steeling herself against his charisma. One look at his dark hair, blue eyes and strong runner's body and her willpower seeped through the soles of her favorite high-heel pumps. *Go figure.*

"I can't talk to you now. We should discuss this with our lawyers present."

A total contradiction of her previous words. Off-balance, surprise and a tinge of outrage ran hotly through her veins, yet she wanted to grab him and lay one on his sexy lips. She wanted to lick along the tail of the dragon winding around one biceps and explore the scaled body tattooed on his shoulder. How could he do this to her?

"I've never cheated on you." Her fault this was playing out publicly, his determined expression told her. He'd wanted to do this in private. The stubborn man didn't move an inch, didn't shift his intent gaze from her. "I haven't slept with a woman since our last time together."

"That's a lie." She'd seen the pictures of him with other women, heard the gossip. Hell, the husband-stealing slut had even spoken to her on the phone. Ryan's cell phone. Anger and betrayal pumped through her again, the wound as fresh as the day he'd broken her heart.

"Caleb, tell her," Ryan said, without moving his gaze off her.

Caleb stepped forward, tall and dark and so much like

Ryan they were often mistaken as brothers instead of friends. Heat suffused her cheeks, memories of the three of them cavorting in bed blindsiding her.

Damn.

Julia closed her eyes, hoping the two men were a fanciful mirage.

Unfortunately, her life lacked magic. When she opened her eyes, Ryan and Caleb still stood right in front of her, silent, stubborn sentinels.

"Why would I believe him?" she demanded. "He's your best friend. He'd lie if you asked him."

"You haven't met Neil and Jeff." Ryan pulled out his phone and pushed speed dial. "Ask them your questions."

"It's true," Caleb said. "Ryan acted like a monk for our entire tour. Now I get it," he added. "We had no idea you were married."

"Hey, Neil. It's Ryan. I'm going to put Julia on the line. Can you answer her questions?" He paused. "You don't need to know her name." Another pause. "Hell, no idea. It's not multi-choice. Just answer whatever she asks you. Tell the truth."

Julia accepted the phone from Ryan, humoring him. "Hello."

"Go on. Ask them anything," Ryan repeated.

She glared at Ryan as she spoke. "Is Ryan a man-slut?"

"Jesus, Julia," Ryan snapped.

"Where's the popcorn?" Maggie asked the room at large.

"This is better than a movie."

"Shush," Connor whispered to his wife. "I don't want to miss anything."

Julia glowered at both of her friends and received unrepentant grins in return. "Well? Are you going to answer my question?"

"The truth?" a low, gravelly voice asked.

"Of course." She wanted to learn the truth, didn't she? The pit of her stomach seemed to fall away while she waited for Neil to speak again.

"Before this last tour, Ryan used to have a lot of women. Women are always throwing themselves at him. This tour was different. He still attended the parties, but he didn't leave with anyone. He didn't let any of the women drape themselves over him unless it was a publicity shot. Nothing too personal during the parties either, even before the mugging."

"What mugging?" Julia asked.

Ryan reached for his cell phone. "Satisfied?" He studied her, silently enforcing his will. "Thanks, man. Yeah, I'll explain when you get back to Auckland." He ended the call.

Julia stared at him for an instant longer. "Who was mugged?"

"That's what I want to know," Christina said, nosy interest in her tone.

"I have never cheated on you. Do you believe me?"

Ryan's face was devoid of his normal humor, his eyes darker and more intense. She studied him, taking in the details she hadn't noted due to her initial shock on seeing him. He'd lost weight, his skin bearing a pallor that was in stark contrast to Caleb's healthy tan. When she studied him more closely, she noticed his jeans hung on him and the corners of his eyes bore lines she was sure hadn't been present during their last meeting.

"What about the woman who answered your phone?"

"Ryan was mugged and someone stole his phone and wallet," Caleb said. "Maybe the thief answered your call."

The excuse seemed too easy, too pat, yet a streak of worry jumped into her mind. He'd been hurt? "When? What happened?"

Ryan grimaced. "It happened about a month after we got to Europe."

A burst of emotion choked her throat. Around the same time she'd lost the baby. She'd cursed him because he hadn't been there for her when she needed him.

Could he be telling the truth?

Julia firmed her resolve and straightened. "As riveting as this conversation is, I need to check on my mother before we hit the club." She turned away from Ryan, needing space to order her thoughts. Her mind had bounced in twenty directions all day. Now Ryan—well he'd taken center stage in typical lead singer fashion.

Someone thumped on the front door. "Probably some

of the staff," she said to Connor. "If it's Stan, our security man, ask him if he'd mind keeping an eye on the door and letting in the rest of the staff as they arrive."

"No problem." Connor ambled away, giving Julia one less thing to worry about.

Julia continued to ignore Ryan and Caleb, paid no heed to the curiosity bubbling through her friends. They'd have questions. Hell, she did, but right now she had to focus. "Susan, I've calculated the wages." She pulled a heavy book out of the bag she'd lugged around all day. "Here's the wage book and the wage packets I did this afternoon. Can you pay everyone as they arrive? Get them to sign for their wages and ask them if they'd mind waiting for a few minutes. I'll speak with them and run through my plans as soon as I've checked on my mother."

Susan wrinkled her freckled nose as she accepted the book and wages. "Your mother runs a manual wage system?" The horror lacing her tone pulled a bark of amusement from Julia.

"We need to get a computer program sorted. It's one of the many things on my list. Tell the staff we'll pay wages by direct credit once we reopen."

Susan nodded. "I'll take care of it."

"What do you want me to do?" Maggie asked.

Christina grabbed Maggie's arm. "We'll take measurements and work out what we need in the way of materials. The chairs need recovering. The tables are awful."

"Thank you." With a grateful nod, Julia started toward her mother's apartment. Footsteps behind her jerked her to an abrupt halt, and she turned to nail the culprit—Ryan—with a glare. "Where are you going?"

"I want to meet your mother." Ryan's brows drew together while his mouth grew tight-lipped. "The miracle mother who has mysteriously returned from the dead."

An uncharacteristic flush suffused her cheeks, and she caught her bottom lip between her teeth, worrying it while she avoided Ryan's gaze. No wonder their marriage hadn't worked. They'd both had secrets, parts of their lives they kept private. That was the trouble with a short courtship and a hurried marriage. Stuff got put off until later.

"I'm gonna hang around and help with measurements," Caleb said with a smart-ass grin. "The chick is right. This is way better than a movie."

"Friends are a pain in the ass," Ryan muttered.

Julia glowered in Caleb's direction. "On that we agree." She stomped up the stairs to her mother's apartment. Earlier, she'd checked on her via phone but Julia wanted to see in person. Soft feminine voices filtered through the door. Ah, good. Janet, her mother's friend, had arrived.

"Why did you lie about your mother?"

Julia whirled around to face Ryan. "Are you still here?"

"I'm not going anywhere."

"Why? Our marriage was a stupid mistake. Just sign the

divorce papers so we can both move on with our lives."

"Damn it, Julia. Our marriage isn't a mistake. Can't you give us a chance? You told me you loved me."

"I—"

The door flew open before she could get out her reply.

"Ah, I thought I heard voices." Janet was a petite brunette, stylish in her black slacks and red and black silk shirt. As usual, she'd boosted her height by teaming her outfit with a pair of gorgeous black shoes with a spike heel. Janet spent a lot of time with Elise and Julia didn't ask nosy questions—not when she was so grateful for Janet's presence.

"Is it Julia?" Elise called.

Janet smiled and gave Julia a swift hug. "Julia and her young man," she called back. "Make sure you're decent. I'm bringing them in."

"I'm Ryan, Julia's husband," Ryan said. "Pleased to meet you."

"We're getting a divorce," Julia snapped, thrown off balance by Ryan's solid presence, his insistence on keeping up the marriage charade.

Ryan placed his hand on the small of her back to shunt her through the doorway, and she couldn't prevent her gasp of shock. His sparse touch generated an electric charge that rocked her to her toes. A healthy dose of heat blossomed where it had no business blooming, and her pulse kicked into a racy beat.

"You'd better come in," Janet said dryly, her gaze darting from her to Ryan and back again with curious fascination.

"Do not tell my mother we're married," Julia ordered in a harsh whisper. Her friends would ask enough questions. Right now they were likely pulling supposition together, speculating. "She has enough to worry about at present without you upsetting her."

"The good news would cheer her up. Not the divorce part," Janet said, winking at them with mascara-laden eyes. "But the fact you're married. She worries about you, Julia. She thinks you hate men."

Julia's mouth opened and closed, another weird flash of heat striking her cheeks at the sound of Ryan's husky laugh. "I do so like men," she said when her wits unscrambled.

"I can vouch for that," Ryan said, arming his cheeky grin with enough charm to win over the grumpiest maiden aunt.

Julia counted to ten under her breath but didn't reach five before she blew. "No one asked you."

Amusement played tag with Janet's lips. "I wasn't implying you were a lesbian. I meant you treat men as commodities and throw them away when you're done."

"And you had the cheek to call me a slut," Ryan said silkily.

Her gaze jerked to him, her mouth opening to refute his charge when she caught the familiar twinkle in his eyes—one that weakened her knees and sent sensations coursing the length of her traitorous body. The one that made her want to jump him.

"What are you whispering about out there?" her mother called. "I might have one foot in the grave but my hearing is still excellent."

Janet stood aside, making shooing motions with her hands. Julia entered her mother's room, each step filled with foreboding. "Mum, how are you?"

"Thanks to you, I had a good night's sleep. Aren't you going to introduce me to your young man?"

Ryan stepped forward before Julia could reply. "I'm Ryan Callander." He swung a glance in her direction, his chin lifting a fraction in challenge.

"Ryan, this is my mother, Elise Maxwell. And you've already met her friend, Janet Wright." She cut across his challenge, barely pausing for a breath as she prayed he wouldn't drop the H bomb again.

"He's her husband," Janet said.

Julia groaned, bracing herself for the inevitable fallout.

"You never told me you were married," her mother said.

Julia swallowed, seeing the hurt in her eyes, hearing it in her chiding voice.

"Are you ashamed of me?" her mother asked. "I thought you'd got past your embarrassment with my occupation."

"I worked here too." Once again, Julia's attention slid to Ryan. She could practically see the questions ticking over in him, and she silently implored him to stem his curiosity.

"It's not Julia's fault," Ryan said. "I asked her not to make any announcements because…well, it's complicated and a long story."

"I'm not going anywhere," her mother said, showing a little of her usual fighting spirit. She struggled to right herself on the pillows, and Ryan was at her side in an instant, assisting her with gentle hands.

"Not tonight," Julia said. *She'd kill him. The minute she got him alone, she was going to kill him.* "I need to talk to you about the club. I've looked at the books, and we need to make changes before we go broke. Are you okay with that?"

Janet and her mother exchanged glances. "We've already talked about a revamp," Janet said. "Elise knows the club is in trouble, but she hasn't had the energy to do anything to get things back on track."

"Do you want me to run things past you before I put them into action?" Julia was surprised by her mother's willingness to let Janet speak for her.

"Janet is a silent partner in the business," Elise said, answering her unspoken question. "It's fine with me as long as Janet agrees."

"If Julia will take responsibility for the club, it means you and I can find somewhere sunny to take a real break for a change." Janet reached over and patted her mother's hand, the action speaking of easy intimacy. "What do you say to that, Elise? As soon as you have clearance from the doctors, we'll book ourselves a holiday on a Pacific Island. Imagine sitting by the pool, sunning ourselves during the day, and watching the sun go down with a cocktail in our hands."

"White sand. The gentle music of waves coming to shore. It sounds wonderful," her mother said with a soft sigh of longing.

"Wait! You're not Elise," Julia said, speechless at her mother agreeing to a holiday. She glanced around the bedroom at the pile of glossy magazines sitting on the bedside cabinet, the dressing table with the crystal bowls and antique hairbrush. "What have you done with my mother?"

"Hilarious," Elise retorted. "The club is all yours. Have at it. Now tell me about this man of yours. How did you meet?"

Ryan followed Julia down the stairs. Her straight back and stiff gait vibrated with fury. She didn't want him here. Too bad. He'd married her for the long haul, and he'd do whatever it took to win her back.

"I should have ignored your advice to keep quiet about our marriage," he said. "I should have argued harder until I convinced you to travel with the band or at least come over to visit me for a few weeks."

"Your manager doesn't want the band members to have

permanent women," she said brusquely. "Wives." She stalked over to her friend, the one with the long straight hair and freckles, who was taking care of the wages. His gaze followed the gentle sway of Julia's hips beneath her tight black trousers before he hurried to catch up.

"And we both know Seymour can't force me to remain single."

She stiffened even further, if that were possible, and swung around to face him. "The way you're carrying on you might as well take an ad out in the newspaper."

Good point. He and the rest of the band didn't want word to get out about their true identities. "Meet me tomorrow for lunch and we can talk."

"I'll have to work here tomorrow."

"You have to eat. I'll grab something and meet you here."

She muttered something under her breath before scowling at him. "Fine."

"Good, it's a date. Since Caleb and I are here, we'll help. Give us an assignment."

She tossed her head, setting her long blonde curls in motion. "Leave."

Caleb jogged across the club to join them and overheard their last words. "You've put your friends to work. What do you want us to do?"

Julia's shoulders drooped. "You're not gonna leave, are you?"

"Nope," Caleb said, grinning in the familiar stir-it-up

way he had.

Ryan remained quiet, happy for his buddy to take the flack. Yep, he'd save the spotlight for a more private time.

"Fine," she muttered again—her go-to word apparently. "Check out the lighting and the stage for me. Tell me what I need to do to upgrade and improve on what's there now."

"You own this place?" Caleb asked.

Respectable job, Caleb. Keep up the quest for information. Ryan knew she did, or rather her mother and friend owned the joint, but he wanted details, fascinated by what he'd learned tonight. He was certain Julia hadn't mentioned a family business, and she'd had ample opportunity to tell him about her mother. He should shout and holler, but he was so damn pleased to see her he couldn't hold onto his irritation.

"My mother owns *The Last Frontier*. It's been in the family for four generations." Her tight-lipped voice hinted at her conflict. She wasn't the prim, uptight type, so he wondered why the club embarrassed her.

"Cool," Caleb said. "Do you strip as well?"

Whoa! Ryan glared at his friend. No one saw his wife naked apart from him.

"I'm a secretary," Julia said in a tight voice. "I don't normally work here."

Caleb raised his hands in surrender. "Just curious. You said nothing when we first met."

Julia's glare darkened. "You two understand lighting.

Give me a verbal report on anything that needs fixing." She wheeled around and stomped away, the slap of her high heels highlighting her annoyance.

"Did you have to wind her up?"

"You wanted answers. I asked the questions for you." Caleb glanced over his shoulder at a burst of feminine laughter. "I told her friends we were roadies with a successful band."

"And?"

"They adore *French Letters*. Their words. They wanted to learn about Dubois and Beauchamp. Their favorites," he said smugly.

At the revelation, a flash of amusement doused some of Ryan's Julia-related anxiety. "Yeah?"

"I said they were assholes but weren't bad singers," Caleb said. "What? I could hardly tell them Beauchamp was standing right in front of them and Dubois is married to their friend. Seymour would kill us for letting out that info."

"You're a pain in my ass." Ryan stalked off toward the stage, grinning when he heard his friend running after him. Secretly he was glad Caleb was here, helping diffuse some of Julia's anger and aiding him as he floundered through unchartered waters.

"She doesn't want a divorce."

"What?" Ryan swung around to face his friend.

"She watches you when you're not looking. You've hurt

her, but it's fixable."

"That's your considered opinion?"

"It is." Caleb's seriousness gave way to a grin of pure evil. "Perhaps I should give you an incentive. If you fuck this up with Julia and let her get away, it will clear the way for me. She likes me a little."

"Don't even consider it," Ryan snarled, possessiveness roaring through him at the idea of someone else with his wife. "Julia gave us a job. We'd better get to it." He climbed the set of pitted steps at the far end of the stage.

"You think I don't mean it. Julia is a sexy woman. She might be the one to make me settle down."

Ryan snorted. "She's my wife."

"Only because you thought of it first."

"Because I'm the intelligent one," Ryan said. "Where the fuck are the lights? It's dark as hell back here."

"Isn't hell full of fires?"

Ryan groaned, more alert and mentally with it than he'd been for months. Caleb, ever the smart-ass. He patted along the wall with his hand. "Ah, I've found the switches." He flicked them and bright light illuminated the stage.

He and Caleb exchanged a look.

"I wonder how the acoustics hold up." Caleb warbled a few notes of a current pop song. "Nice. Are you thinking what I'm thinking?"

"Yeah," Ryan said. "We get a place to practice that's out

of the public radar, and I get to hang out with my wife."

"Good plan."

"I liked it," Ryan said.

"What about Julia's friends? Won't they wonder why we're playing music?"

"We'll tell them we got the bug and are starting our own band. Besides, we're writing new songs. If we play an oldie, they'll think we're doing a cover."

Caleb smirked. "I never knew you were so devious."

"Whatever it takes to win back Julia," Ryan said.

Whatever it takes.

"Julia! Where did you meet two roadies? They've worked with *French Letters*," Christina said, excitement making her bounce around like a kid. The motion set her multitude of bracelets jingling.

"Did they say how long they were back in Auckland before they head off again?" she asked in an attempt at casual.

Christina and Maggie both stared at her. "Don't you know?"

"We're getting a divorce. It's none of my business," Julia said.

"He doesn't want a divorce," Maggie said. "I think he's cute."

"Connor, your wife is lusting after my husband," Julia shouted.

Maggie clicked her fingers in Julia's face, her satisfaction veering close to smugness. "So you admit he's yours." She sobered. "Was he the father.?"

"I don't want to talk about that," Julia snarled, her teeth bared in a heart-pounding flash of rage. "And if you tell him I'll never speak to you again."

Maggie's humor faded and she backed away, her hands held up in a gesture of surrender. "Julia, I'd never do that to you. I'm sorry I mentioned it. It was a bad joke. I didn't mean to upset you."

Anguish filled Julia then, the feelings she'd tried to stuff in the pockets of her mind jumping front and center. The fury at Ryan, at herself for losing their child. The accursed guilt that never seemed to go away. Why had Ryan crashed back into her life? She'd pulled herself back together, and now that he'd appeared every bad memory seemed brand new again. She sucked in a breath, battling the need to blubber. God, she was turning into a crybaby. Her hands clenched the clipboard like a lifeline.

She wondered how long Ryan was back for this time. *French Letters* was doing well on the charts. Surely it wouldn't be too long before they headed off on tour and her life could return to normal.

Julia's glance hit the stage and landed on Ryan and Caleb. Or as normal as it could be for the manager of an ailing strip club.

CHAPTER FOUR

"I NEED TO CHECK in with Susan and get the staff meeting underway." Julia strode away from Maggie.

Have you no shame, woman? Stop looking at his arse.

The vibes from her skeleton staff weren't encouraging, but she pinned on a friendly smile. "Thank you for coming," she said, studying the faces of the women clustered around the bar. "I've gone over the books and this is what I propose. We'll close for two weeks while we do a facelift on the place." She ran through the rest of her plans for the club. "While the club is shut, I'll need help with painting and some of the other stuff. I'll also do rehearsals for stripping and burlesque. Before you go tonight, let me know if you want to keep working here or if you intend to hand in your notice. Questions?"

"What about pay?" one woman asked.

"Those who come in to help and turn up for rehearsals

will receive their regular pay."

"I can't survive without my tips," the woman said.

"From what I saw last night, tips are few and far between," Julia said briskly. "I'll pay your base wage. Once we open again I hope we'll bring in more punters, and everyone will receive tips."

"A facelift is all very well." The woman's weary features held defiance. The heavy lines fanning from the corner of her eyes and mouth hinted at a hard life. Her voice rasped with the undertones of a heavy smoker. "But why the hell should we trust you? You're young. A secretary, I hear. What the hell do you know about running a strip club?"

Julia met the woman's gaze and understood she'd need to prove herself, to respond to the opposition. Wheeling about, she caught Ryan staring. A ripple of awareness shot the length of her body, irritating the hell out of her. She felt nothing for the rat. *She. Did. Not.*

She stalked over to him. "Cue some music for me, please. Can you manage that?" Her voice was icy and held distinct challenge. She held back a tiny snort of amusement at her behavior. *Bitch, anyone?*

"Anything in particular?" Ryan asked.

"Something up-tempo." Julia made her way onto the stage, aware everyone was watching her. The women on the staff nudged each other, most still wearing their belligerent expressions. To them she was the interloper, the daughter who'd decided she could fix everything—the educated 'ideas' person who excelled at theory but had no field experience.

The first strains of a rock ballad flooded the club, one of *French Letters'* top ten hits. *How apt.* Julia didn't give in to the temptation to glance in Ryan's direction. The wretched man knew this was her favorite song. He'd sung it to her one night after they'd made love, their sweaty limbs still tangled together. The song—it held memories.

Julia closed her eyes to absorb the beat of the music, then opened them again as experience came to the fore, placing her firmly in the stripper mindset. She grinned, arching her back and gripping the pole in front of her for balance. Gazes fastened on her swaying body and followed the subtle twists of her shoulders, her hips, shooting prickling awareness through her. Ryan was watching her. She faltered for an instant.

Concentrate, stupid. This is about proving your point.

The length of her leg slid along the pole as she gripped it and tipped upside down. Confidence flooded her again, and she moved fluidly, as if she'd been dancing all along. Gliding sinuously to the *French Letters'* tune, she righted herself and winked at the gawking group, changing the mood of the dance into fun and flirty.

She strutted away from the gleaming pole, her fingers trailing up and down the placket of her blouse. One by one, she released her buttons, slowly revealing her curves, working it. A shoulder shrug here. A hip roll there. A few minutes later, her expensive blouse hit the floor.

A sharp whistle cut the air. Connor smirked at her while Maggie rose on tiptoe to clap her hands over his eyes.

Julia continued, determined to prove to her employees she understood what she was doing. Each move was sensuous, calculated and designed to inflame those watching the act—both male and female. The removal of her trousers wasn't elegant, but she did her best, fluttering her eyelashes and pursing her lips at her audience. The fabric slipped down her legs, and she stepped free. Thank goodness for the wide-legged style.

Unhindered by clothing, she sashayed back to the pole, her breasts heaving with exertion. She ran through another sequence of gyrations, twisting and turning, dipping and arching her body into positions designed to entice. Entertain.

As the music passed the climax and slammed to an end, she upped her pace, spinning and hugging the pole, flowing into some of her showier tricks. Julia used the music and when it crashed into the finale, she held her final pose, chest rising and falling rapidly, blood rushing through her veins.

Silence fell.

Julia slid from the pole, scooped up her shirt and trousers and sauntered back to face her employees in just her matching lacy underwear. She was aware of the pleasure flooding her body, the buzz of exhilaration.

Although she'd walked away from the occupation, it was obvious—to her at least—that showmanship ran through her blood. Her father's family had told the truth. She was as common as her mother.

A round of applause broke out, her friends leading the charge.

"Any questions?" she asked crisply, purposely refraining from checking Ryan's reaction.

"I'm in," Maggie shouted from the left. "Lessons and everything."

Julia scanned the faces, homing in on the woman who'd challenged her. "Do you have any other concerns?"

The woman shook her head, poker face in place. "You've surprised me, and that doesn't happen often, but I've got kids to feed. I can't wait around until you get the club running again."

"Fair enough." Julia wasn't about to argue. She needed a team who stood behind her in everything. Men and women open to change and innovative ideas, because that's what it'd take to get this club back to the stage where the punters queued, willing to wait to gain admittance.

"If we hang around while the club is closed, are we guaranteed our jobs?" It was the barmaid, and she sucked noisily on a lollypop while she waited for an answer.

"I might reshuffle positions," Julia said without hesitation. "Everyone will receive training, and I'll assess your strengths and weaknesses—"

"If you intend to do any of that touchy-feely shit businesses do to bond their staff, I'm out of here," the barmaid said.

"That's your prerogative," Julia said.

The lollypop bulged in one cheek. "Huh?"

"She means you need to make up your own mind," one stripper murmured.

"If there are no other questions, you're free to go. Please let Susan know if you intend to continue with your employment here or, if you prefer, you can stop by tomorrow morning and tell me then. Those of you who wish to remain, please arrive at nine tomorrow morning. We'll work office hours until the club reopens."

"You can pull your tongue in now," Ryan said with a glance at Caleb. "And get your eyes off my wife's arse."

"Wow," Caleb said. "Did you realize she could do that?"

"No," Ryan said, torn between wanting to stare hungrily at her exposed flesh—because she hadn't pulled on her clothes again—and wanting to rush over and cover her long limbs and torso with a... He glanced around for something suitable. A curtain might do the job. "My wife has hidden talents."

"I'm only going to Tauranga for the weekend," Caleb said.

Ryan ripped his gaze off Julia to stare at his friend. "What? Why? You told your parents you were going for an entire week."

"This is way too good to miss. Besides, I want to help. They're going to paint and stuff. We can do that. We can help sort out the lighting and the stage props, and since you already have so many songs done, we can get a head start on the arrangements."

"One condition," Ryan said, turning back to watch Julia. God, she was so beautiful. He'd already known she was bright and intelligent, but now he was seeing it in action, and it was damn sexy.

"What's that?"

"You stop flirting with my wife."

"Nope," Caleb said. "I've decided I have a thing for troublesome women. I need to keep you honest. Besides, if she kicks your sorry ass to the footpath, I want to be on the spot to grab my chance."

Ryan snorted rudely. "Julia is mine, and I have the marriage certificate to prove it. We'd better finish our assignment and make ourselves indispensable, otherwise both our arses will leave skid marks along the pavement."

"We could help her out with finances," Caleb said.

"I've considered offering money, but I don't want to injure her pride."

"We can offer to pay for rehearsal space."

"Yeah, that might work. I'll run the idea past her tomorrow." He considered Julia's sexy stage routine and smiled. "I have an idea for another song. Two, actually."

"Spill. Wait. It's not a ballad is it?"

"One of each," Ryan said, excitement pounding through him. This was a way to help Julia, something concrete to assist her with the club—a special theme song by *French Letters*. There must be a way to swing something so the band wasn't outed because he wanted to help.

Caleb played with the lights, testing the different spotlights and the color filters. Ryan watched with a critical eye.

"She won't need to do much with the lighting. The wiring and everything looks good," Caleb said, after peering into the switchbox and prodding a few things.

"The curtain and some of the props they have back here need renewing. They're tacky and old." Ryan tapped a large metal birdcage, big enough for a person, and a cloud of dust rose. He backed away before he sneezed.

"You want to report to Julia?" Caleb asked.

"Yeah."

Ryan appreciated Caleb giving him space and the opportunity of a few private words with her. He practiced what he'd say in his mind while he searched the club for her. He ran her to ground in the stock room where she was doing an inventory of the booze with one of her friends. "Hey."

"Damn, that's bad timing," the friend said. "I was about to grill her about you."

"Why don't you ask me?" he asked.

"Ryan." Julia scowled at him, an expression he'd noticed

her wearing a lot tonight.

He tut-tutted. "Didn't your mother warn you the changing wind can fix a frown in place? Your smile is much sexier."

The friend laughed, despite Julia's deepening glower.

"I'm Ryan," he said, sticking out his hand. He flicked a glance in Julia's direction. "Julia's husband."

"Maggie," she said. "Connor's wife."

"The big dude who can't keep his eyes off you?"

"That would be the one," she said with a fond grin.

"Julia, can we talk?"

"I'll leave you alone," Maggie said, brushing past Julia.

"No," Julia blurted, her hand snapping out to grip her friend's arm.

"Julia," Maggie protested.

"Why don't I tell you about the sound and lighting system first," Ryan said, watching his wife glance at the door with longing. Now dressed, she appeared cool, armor in place. Damn, he'd hurt her. Seeing Julia had brought back forgotten memories and filled some gaps. After they'd married, she'd told him of some of her past with boyfriends, joked about her bad luck until she met him. Now she'd consigned him to the top of the male scrapheap and donned her bitchy manner to conceal her pain. To set her at ease, he plunged into the conclusions he and Caleb had come to regarding the current setup.

"So we can get by with cosmetic fixes on the curtains and

props?" she asked.

"That's good news," Maggie said. "Six bottles of vodka."

"Six? Damn, the vodka is short too. Someone has been helping themselves to the booze." Julia jotted down the number against the computer-generated stock list.

"Ah, heck. Look at the time," Maggie said. "We need to hit the other club before the line gets too long. I'll tell the others." She sped off, leaving Ryan clear to speak in private with Julia.

"I don't want to listen to anything you have to say," Julia said.

"Please, hear me out. The mugging story is true. While we were in Munich, I was attacked. Three guys were hassling a woman and I stopped to help. After I escorted her home, the guys jumped me, beat me up pretty bad." He paused, trying to dig the rusty facts from his swirling head. "I was left with short-term memory loss. It's taken a while to remember things."

Her stiff manner dispersed a fraction. "Are you okay now?"

"Some of my memories are still fuzzy. I didn't remember you straight away."

"That's good for my ego," Julia said drily.

"Do you think this has been fun for me? I remembered our songs. We had to cancel one concert, but until I returned home and checked my mail, I only recalled your first name. The divorce papers were a rude awakening."

She cocked her head to the side, her expression unreadable. "You didn't tell Caleb about your marriage?"

"You asked me not to." Ryan held her gaze, wanting to reach out and touch her in the worst way. "Remember your long lecture about wanting to maintain your privacy and avoid nosy questions from reporters and ladies' magazines? I still say you wouldn't get much of that because we're anonymous offstage." His gaze traced the high cheekbones, her straight nose and the curve of her full lips. A zip of heat struck his groin, and a rush of memories bombarded him—crystal clear and perfect. Of making love to her, her mouth on him. Those lips of hers were something else. "You didn't tell your friends either."

"No." Something dark swirled in her eyes for a second. Maybe regret?

"I don't want a divorce, Julia. I want this marriage. I want you."

She swallowed, focusing on the paper clutched in her hands. "I can't do a long-distance marriage. I thought it would be okay, but..." She trailed off, still not looking at him.

"We're home for a few months," he said. "Seymour wants us to write new material and record another album. Couldn't we start again? Face our problems together without secrets this time?"

"I can't." Pain carried in the hoarse whisper, and she seemed to zone out for an instant. Then she glanced at him, the sheen of emotion welling in her eyes. "I don't think I'm good with relationships."

He'd done this to her. The hurt radiating from her weakened his knees. Before he'd realized it, he had gathered her in his arms. When she tipped back her head, a tear escaped, and he brushed it away with his thumb. She surrendered, the paper and pen dropping to the floor. Her arms wrapped around his neck, and she pressed her face to his shirt, a tremble rippling through her slender body.

Ryan dragged in a deep breath, his anxiety lessening now that he held her. This was home. Now all he had to do was convince her.

"Julia." He breathed her in, the floral and herbal notes of her perfume, familiar and comforting even though he struggled to recall the name of the scent.

She lifted her head, and he was totally lost. He claimed her mouth softly, hesitating in case she rejected him. Relief struck him hard when her hands tightened on his shirt, but he kept the kiss casual, licking her lips and relearning her taste.

Sweet. Beautiful.

His.

He shivered at the surge of heat racing to his groin and desperately attempted to quell the blast of sexual need. *Slow and easy.* Gradually, he deepened the kiss, drinking in her sweetness, allowing his body to tell her everything—how much he'd missed her, hungered for her even when he hadn't remembered her name.

He'd known his mystery woman was important, instinctively realized he had to keep the memory to himself until he'd worked everything through. If only he'd come home after the accident. But he'd had commitments and he'd honored them.

"Julia," he whispered. "I love you."

She thrust away from him without warning, leaving him bereft. "You forget. I saw the photos of you with other women."

"Show them to me," he said, not willing to back down or walk away from this important fight. "Are you sure they weren't digitally altered? Neil and Caleb have both vouched for me. I haven't slept with another woman since I left New Zealand."

"That you recollect." Her expression held skepticism.

"I remember cold showers. Many cold showers." The memory went some way to cooling his ardor, for which he was thankful. The last thing he needed was for her to think he only wanted her for sex. "I spent a lot of my free time writing new songs," he said. "I can show you the songs. Caleb and I have worked on the arrangements. Please give me a chance. Let me prove myself." Words almost tumbled over each other as he sought a way through her anger, her doubt. "Please."

"I'm going to be busy with the club," she said.

"Let me help. Caleb and I were talking earlier. The

acoustics are excellent, and it would make a suitable place for us to rehearse our new material. Somewhere off the radar. We'd pay you for use of the space."

He had no idea what he'd do if she refused. Nah, that was a lie. Even if he had to camp outside with a guitar and play songs on the street, he'd spend his hours with her, attempting to change her mind.

"All right," she said after a long pause, her tone grudging. "But you're not moving in with me."

His held breath released with a hiss. Okay. He could work with that. "Will you let me take you to dinner?"

"Maybe."

"All right." A maybe was as good as a yes. "And the band can rehearse here?"

"Are you sure that's a good idea? What about my friends and the staff? What are you going to tell them? I presume you want to keep your identities quiet?"

He didn't care. He'd make this work. "Caleb has already told them we work as roadies. We'll keep to the story and tell them we're contemplating forming a band with some friends. Even if we play *French Letters* music, they'll think we're doing covers of popular music. Most people see what they want. Without our stage makeup, no one recognizes us."

Julia nodded, losing some of her starchiness. "If anyone asks I'll tell them you're a band looking for a break."

"Julia, are you ready?" Maggie shouted.

"Are you and Caleb coming to the club with us?" Julia asked, gliding around him in a wide circle. "We're checking out the opposition."

"Thanks." Satisfaction filled his chest, and despite her strictures about taking things slowly, he was quietly pleased. She reminded him of the dog his family had adopted from the Humane Society when he was a kid. Despite her feisty attitude, she acted as if he might kick her at the first opportunity. Troublesome wench. That dog had become his best buddy, and he intended to use the same calm persistence with his wife.

The hour was still early—in club terms—yet already a line had formed outside. The seven of them joined the end of the queue, keeping the conversation away from *The Last Frontier*. A burly bouncer, dressed in a black suit, stood at the head of the line, his massive arms crossed over his chest. His bring-it-on size shouted a warning for everyone to behave, but none of the waiting people were interested in issuing a challenge.

"Have you been here before?" Julia asked the couple standing in front of them. She wanted to get a feel for the clientele and learn what attracted them to this new club. Anything to get her mind off Ryan. God, she'd let him kiss her, which ranked right up there with stupid. Sly, tricky man. His gentleness had cut her mental arguments off at the knees and fogged her stupid brain.

"Good music. Great atmosphere," a woman said. "There are both male and female performers so the place doesn't have a sleazy club vibe. It's comfortable here with my girlfriends."

"That's what I heard." Julia surveyed the woman and those in front of them. The dress-code seemed on the casual side for the men, but most of the women were dolled up in skimpy dresses or clinging skirts and flimsy tops. She was glad they'd all taken the chance to smarten up.

"I haven't been here before," Ryan said. "Is the music live or do they have a DJ?"

"DJ," the woman said. "He's good."

Music swirled out when the door opened. Julia didn't recognize the song, but it had a strong beat, something people could dance to if they had the inclination. The bouncer let several people inside, including the woman she'd questioned.

"That's all," the bouncer said, stopping Julia.

"Isn't it unusual to restrict numbers this early in the night?" she asked.

"Not my fault," the bouncer said in a surprisingly high voice, immediately on the defensive.

"Of course it isn't," she said soothingly, leaning toward him to highlight her breasts. "What are the owners like? I might apply for a job."

"Dancer?"

"Yes," Julia said, blinking her eyelashes in his direction. "I wanted to check out the place first. I've been burned before."

Maggie shifted a fraction beside her. Julia caught a masculine growl of disapproval, and she was sure Connor wasn't the culprit.

"I don't think they're hiring at present," the bouncer said, noticeably thawing. "You should check at the bar."

"Thanks. I will."

A group of six men walked out the door, their dark suits indicating they'd hit the place after a day of work. Interesting. Most clubs didn't attract this clientele. What were they doing that was so different?

"How many are in your group?" the bouncer asked.

"Seven," Julia said.

"Close enough. You can go in now. Good luck with the job."

"Thanks." Julia flashed a smile and sashayed into the club, putting an extra wiggle in her hips. It was the least she could do in exchange for the information.

"Hey," Ryan's arm curved around her waist. "I hope your sexy flounce is for me."

Her steps became jerky, and he chuckled. She swallowed, knocked off her usual even stride. His arm felt natural around her, damn it. She'd softened naturally, leaning into his warmth. And that was stupid, but right now she was so confused and out of kilter she had difficulty thinking straight.

"Relax."

"Easy for you to say," she said. "You don't have four curious friends trying to grill you for answers. Or a husband who decides he can walk right back into my life when it suits him."

Ryan's arm tightened as he guided her into the intimacy of the dimly lit club. "This isn't easy for me either."

The tense note in his voice had her searching his face. All this time she'd believed him the bad guy, but what if he spoke the truth? She should own some of the problems with their marriage. She'd seen online pictures almost as soon as the band arrived in Europe, and a part of her had died when they kept appearing. Then the baby... The guilt had overwhelmed her, withering her emotions, plunging her into darkness.

"Meet me for breakfast," she said.

"Where? When?"

"I thought I'd grab something at the cafe down the road from the club. They always used to do a decent breakfast. I want to get an early start."

"Good idea," Maggie said, overhearing them.

"Julia and I are having a private breakfast," Ryan said.

Maggie's lips twitched. "You can share a table together."

Julia got it, and a bloom of emotion warmed her through. In their unsubtle way her friends were telling Ryan they had her back. "Fine," she said, squeezing Ryan's hand to still his protest. "Maggie is right. I have a lot to do, and I can't afford distractions."

"Fine." He threw her reply back at her. "We'll share a table at breakfast, but I get a goodnight kiss."

"That sounds fair," Maggie said, puckering up in Ryan's direction.

"Only if you want a spanking," Connor said sternly.

"Yes, please." Maggie smirked at her husband, one eye closing in a sexy wink.

Susan clapped her hands over her ears. "La, la, la, la."

Julia laughed at Ryan's confusion. "I'll explain later."

"There's a booth," Caleb said. "We should be able to squeeze in there."

"Quick," Christina said. "Let's grab it before the people behind us get the same idea." She took off, gliding between the chairs and tables with real speed.

Ryan's hand slipped from around Julia's waist, and she registered the loss straight away. Damn it. She couldn't act this way. She wasn't a pushover, yet with Ryan... *Focus, girl. This is a business jaunt.*

"I don't understand why they're restricting admission when there are loads of empty tables," Susan said.

"They're playing head games," Caleb said. "If prospective customers see a line outside a club, they think exclusivity. The owners are playing the snob factor and it's working for them."

They crowded into the booth. Julia found herself

squeezed against Ryan.

"Relax," he whispered, slipping his arm around her shoulders. "I only bite in private."

It was privacy that worried her. He'd burst into her life again today, and already she was toast. Well done, burned to a crisp, toast, her emotions and anger warring with her need to run her hands over his shoulder and tattoo to make sure he was real.

Susan pulled out a notebook and pen. "Observations? Points to remember and discuss later?"

"The staff wears a uniform," Christina said. "It's a little blatant for my taste. Uniforms are a clever idea, but they need to aim for sexy and stylish rather than tarty."

"Music is good," Caleb contributed. "Lighting is okay, but not very original."

"That might change once an exotic dancer comes on stage," Maggie said.

"Service is slow," Connor said. "I'll go to the bar. What does everyone want to drink?"

"Wine," Julia said.

"Let's get a bottle of Sav Blanc," Maggie suggested.

The music changed and a dramatic drum roll burst through the speakers. A spotlight highlighted a short, slim man dressed in an elegant navy suit. "Let me present, fresh from the Las Vegas club circuit, Garnet!"

The spotlight faded, blacking out the man's presence. The music changed to subtle and flirty. Tension gripped

Julia, herds of butterflies dive-bombing her stomach, trying to work their way out. What if she couldn't do this? What if she was wasting her efforts on an old dame who was way past her prime?

A red spotlight appeared center stage, highlighting a woman dressed in a dazzling black gown. The woman started to sing, dancing and moving in an enticing manner. A cock of her hips. A pout of plump red lips. She was good with an excellent voice, but Julia thought she could hold her own in a strip off. The singing, not so much, but in the dancing and stripping Julia decided she had an edge.

"You're better," Ryan murmured.

"Are you sure? I can't carry a tune."

"That doesn't matter. Lip-syncing will work if it's done properly. Besides, you don't want to copy them. You need to work out your own business plan and stick to it."

He was right, she thought, her panic receding. She needed to work on the plans she and her friends had discussed, the ideas she'd had as a teenager and her mother had rejected. This was her chance to put her stamp on the club. First up, she'd rename the club *Maxwell's* in honor of her great-grandparents. A strip club might have been shameful during Victorian times, but social mores changed. If she marketed the place as classy, she'd attract the right customers.

"We need a motto or a tag line for the club," Julia said.

"I thought *The Last Frontier* said it all," Susan said.

"I'm talking about *Maxwell's*," Julia said. "A different vintage all together."

"Nice," Maggie said. "Stylish."

"Perfect," Ryan said.

"What about Hollywood glamour as a theme?" Christina asked, leaning across the table to be heard. "Perhaps even a hint of Art Deco."

"What sort of theme does this place have?" Connor asked.

"It's cozy and intimate, but the furnishings are bland." Christina dissected the club's interior with an artist's eye. "They've played it safe. You need to deliver an experience for your customers. Something they'll talk about for weeks after the event—in a good way. Get the word-of-mouth thing going."

Excitement flared inside Julia. Her friends were right. Myriad clubs had opened and closed on K' Road over the years. Her mother's club had weathered the competition and remained an institution. Now it was time to reinvent and carve out a new niche.

"You're excited by the challenge," Ryan murmured.

Yes. Yes, she was. "I can do this."

"I had no doubts. Look at your friends. They don't have an ounce of uncertainty either. We're on your team, Julia."

Julia coughed delicately to shift the growing lump lodged in her windpipe. He might be right when it came to the club, but he'd have to go back on the road with the band. They'd be separated because the club would keep her tethered to Auckland.

"Don't," he whispered. "I can hear you thinking. This marriage will work. I won't see it any other way."

"Theory is fine. It's the practical things that'll make a relationship between us difficult." She winced, emotion a tight fist interfering with her heartbeat. "What about children?" *Oh, god. What was she doing?*

His brows drew together, gentle fingers tipping up her chin, forcing her to meet his direct gaze. "You want children?"

A familiar pain gripped her, losing her baby tormenting her like an infected tooth. She forced out a light laugh and managed quite well. No one would guess her feelings, the despondency still hiding bone deep in her soul. No, she'd never wanted children—not until she'd discovered she was pregnant.

His expression changed, making her realize she'd hesitated too long. He'd deciphered her silence as negative. She hurried into speech. "We never discussed children."

"No." His eyes narrowed on her in silent regard, but luckily he didn't ask questions or poke at the barely scabbed wound. "We didn't discuss a lot of things. I'm looking forward to learning more about you and making up the deficit."

"Besides, children wouldn't work with you on tour." She fell silent, aware she was laboring the topic, yet unable to stop herself.

His stare forced the creep of heat up her neck. *Yeah, stupid!* She should have kept her big mouth firmly shut. "What do you think of the club? What are they doing that Mum isn't at *The Last Frontier*?"

"The exclusive vibe seems to work for them. The service is adequate, but not perfect. Ambiance is okay—nothing special or memorable, but the presenter is a nice touch. Their dancer isn't as good as you, but everyone seems to appreciate her act." He gestured toward a table of men, most in their early twenties.

His summation of facts, the same observations she'd already assimilated in her mind let some of her panic retreat.

"How long did you work for your mother at the club?"

Her stress levels took off again, soaring to breath-stealing heights. The minute someone learned of her past, they treated her differently. Mention the words exotic dancer and most minds took the straight leap to sex and prostitution. While she wasn't ashamed of stripping, she didn't broadcast it either.

Connor returned with a tray of drinks, thankfully interrupting their quiet discussion. She accepted a glass of wine with a smile and set it down while glancing around the club, jumping deeper into analyzing mode.

"Julia, you haven't answered my question." Ryan's quiet insistence had her reaching for her glass.

She took a healthy swig, offering little respect to the crisp notes of summer fruit. Her stomach churned as she took a second sip. Irritation layered on top of her panic and fear, and an outrageous thought struck her. Hell, prevarication wasn't working. Why shouldn't she hit him with the truth? "I worked at the club from the age of sixteen."

"Sixteen, but that's—"

"Underage," she interrupted. "I know, but I needed money to pay for clothes and secretarial courses. I had to save because my mother put in everything she had to pay off the mortgage on the place. I worked at the club and left once I turned nineteen." She damned up the spill of words and waited for his horrified reaction, waited for him to conclude he'd married a prostitute. Even now, the taunts from kids at primary school burned her ears. She recalled in excruciating detail every hushed conversation from her school friends' parents. Yeah, she'd learned firsthand how people judged.

It shouldn't matter if Ryan formed the same opinion as others but it did. When he'd asked her to marry him, she'd considered a confession and finally talked herself into not saying anything. The why of her decision became important now. Her breath whooshed out, her streak of honesty kicking her on the butt.

She'd loved Ryan and hadn't wanted to risk losing him. The irony of it was she'd lost him anyway.

CHAPTER FIVE

Ryan insisted on escorting her home. At the entrance to her apartment building, he kissed her on the cheek before leaving in the cab with Caleb. Once again, he confused her with his behavior. He was unpredictable, still mesmerizing. Drat it! She shoved him from her mind, going through her usual pre-bed routine.

Three hours later, she roamed her apartment unable to sleep because her thoughts ran around a track with no finish line in sight. Ryan. The club. The hundred and one things on her to-do list.

And secrets. God, those secrets kept beating her over the head with a pointy stick.

Exasperated, she grabbed a notepad and pen. If she couldn't sleep at least she'd manage a jump-start on the things she needed to do during the coming weeks. Her pen flew across the page, bullet points and ideas filling the white space.

Then her mind drifted in Ryan's direction and the way they'd first met. Fate, Ryan had called it, and she—the woman with stars in her eyes—had agreed with every word. Yeah, it had all started at the pub. She'd been sitting alone, pondering her next move.

"Surely it can't be that bad?" a male voice had broken through her reverie.

Julia's head had jerked up, ready to tell the guy to piss off. Her sharp words died when her first glance stole her breath. Tall, with dark, slicked back hair and laughing blue eyes, he stood before her full of confidence. A black T-shirt stretched across his muscular chest. Blue jeans, faded at the stress points, completed his casual outfit. Bemused, she let her gaze linger before raising her eyes to meet his cocky grin.

"You have no idea." Julia snorted when a tingle of acute anticipation struck her hard—the beginning thrill of the ritual dance between male and female. Curse her randy hormones. One glance at his confident face made her suspect the way her night would end. Amusement filled her as she imagined Susan's disapproving reaction. So, shoot her. She found a man with self-confidence sexy.

"I'm Ryan and this is Caleb. Can we buy you a drink?"

Her gaze slid to the second man, who stood beside his friend. They were a similar height and build, but Caleb's black hair was longer, a leather band holding it off his face in a ponytail. Two cuties. Maybe she would hold the loneliness at bay.

"Thanks, I'd enjoy that. I'll have a glass of Pinot Gris." She indicated the vacant chairs at her table. "I'm Julia. Have a seat."

"You are alone, right?" Caleb's deep voice stroked across her like delicate fingertips, and she suppressed a moan as desire sped through her body, danced through her veins and coalesced into a spark of promise in her sex.

"As of tonight," she confirmed. "My boyfriend and I had a disagreement about his proclivity for chatting up other women. I don't like to share."

Ryan's dark brows rose. "Never?"

"Ryan, I'll grab the drinks. You want a beer?"

"Please." Ryan never took his gaze off her. She'd always believed pale blue eyes cold. His glowed with intimacy and secrets and a hint of cockiness, and she barely resisted the urge to squirm as he directed that power on her. "You never share?"

She hesitated. She'd never stressed about sleeping with a man on the first date—not if it seemed right. Tonight, her gut was telling her this man was a good catch. His friend too. Julia took a leap of faith and played along. She didn't have to leave the pub with them.

"I might, under the right circumstances." She thought about playing coy, but that wasn't her. Most men seemed to appreciate her straight approach. "We're talking about a threesome, right? You're both good-looking," she continued, not giving him a chance to respond. "Why don't you find a girl each? Why are you willing to share?"

"Because we noticed you at the same time," Caleb said, setting three drinks on the table. "We're only in town for tonight."

"Is that a line?"

"No," Ryan said. "It's the truth. If you're interested in sex, we're your men."

"Or you can choose one of us," Caleb said, settling on the chair beside her.

A startled laugh came from Julia. "Don't you believe in sugarcoating the truth? A little light flirtation first?"

"We can flirt if you like, but the truth is we saw you and wanted you," Ryan said.

"What if I say no? Will you leave me alone again? Hit on another woman?"

"Nah," Caleb said.

"We'll stay for as long as you then go home." Ryan sipped his beer, and fascinated, she watched his throat move when he swallowed. "We can do without sex."

Her gaze drifted from one man to the other, inquisitiveness raising questions. Some men were precious when it came to questions about their manhood.

"What?" Caleb asked.

"You don't...ah...you know." Her hands waved through the air in lieu of words when she chickened out on asking the gay question.

"Do Ryan and I fuck each other?" Caleb chuckled, unperturbed.

"Yeah, that's what I was trying to ask."

"Nope," Ryan said, the appearance of faint laugh lines around his eyes betraying his amusement. "We've shared women, but that's as close as we get."

Caleb winked at her. "I know his bad habits. There's no way I could overlook his snoring."

"I don't snore," Ryan protested.

It was easy to see the two men were close and comfortable in their skins. The confidence thing again—it got her every time. "How long have you known each other?"

"Since we were five," Ryan said.

"And you've been friends ever since?"

Caleb shrugged, his muscular shoulders attracting her attention. "We have a lot in common."

"So what do you do?" Julia decided the normal getting-to-know-you questions would work as well as flirting and giggling. She assumed what they wanted. The question was did she want the same thing.

"We're in sales," Ryan said.

"Selling what?"

Caleb grimaced. "Entertainment. Music mainly, but don't make us talk about work. It's the weekend."

"Time for recreation," Ryan added in a husky voice.

Julia laughed, amused by the pair and already stepping past temptation into certainty. Ryan and Caleb pushed all the right buttons on her libido. "What did you think of the band tonight?"

"They're going places," Caleb said. "I understand they're popular in Australia."

A grin hovered around Ryan's mouth. "What did you think?"

"I want to jump the lead singer." Julia clapped her hand over her mouth, her eyes widening at her blurted thoughts.

A moment of startled silence followed before Ryan and Caleb chortled.

"Why didn't you proposition him? He might have said yes," Caleb said.

"Please," Julia said. "I bet half the females in the pub tried something suggestive on one of those guys. Their disguises are a masterstroke. It keeps everyone guessing, and when they hit the big time, they'll have their anonymity."

Ryan cocked his head. "You think they're that good?"

"I do. No one talked over the music tonight. That's a sign of better than good, and their sex appeal doesn't hurt either."

"We'd better pay attention, Ryan. The lady has spoken, and her tip might come in handy with our job."

Ryan winked, and sexual awareness tugged at Julia's nipples. His grin spread the glide of invisible fingers over her body, and a tremor of pleasure worked down her spine. Her breath caught. She intended to do this—sleep with two attractive strangers.

THEIR APARTMENT SURPRISED HER with its tidiness. Caleb picked up a remote from the arm of a battered sofa and the mellow sounds of a fifties ballad filled the room.

"Would you like to dance?" Ryan tugged her into his arms before she replied, and she automatically fell into step with him. The music didn't fit her expectations either. That would teach her to make snap judgments.

"Fifties music?" she asked.

A body moved behind her and another set of masculine hands touched her, cupping her hips gently as he swayed to the rhythm. Julia relaxed, enjoying the music and the two hard male bodies corralling her.

"It's one of the things we have in common," Ryan murmured against her ear. "We enjoy music from different eras."

Ryan lowered his head to kiss the corner of her mouth. Caleb rubbed his body against her arse. Both men had erections, and the knowledge sent a bolt of lust spearing to her pussy. Her hands wandered under shirts, over bare skin, mapping Ryan's shoulders, tracing the tattoo that disappeared under his T-shirt sleeve and testing Caleb's biceps. She licked Ryan's lips, encouraging him to open for her. The crisp taste of beer and a spicy masculine flavor hit her taste buds, and her fingers curled into his shoulders, forcibly holding her to him.

Behind her, Caleb nuzzled her neck, his warm mouth sucking and nibbling. A nip of teeth sent a jolt of pain through her, the stroke of a tongue soothing the tender spot. A shiver followed on the heels of the sting, resulting in increased moisture between her thighs. He'd leave a mark, but she didn't care. This amount of pleasure was worth the price of a little ribald teasing from her friends during the coming days.

Then she ceased to think about anything except the feelings surging through her hypersensitive body. Ryan's lips and tongue stroked hers, seduced and tempted her. Caleb's hands slid beneath the silky midnight blue fabric of her camisole top, his callused fingertips dragging sensually over her warm skin. His hands moved higher until they nudged the undersides of her breasts. Her imagination did the rest, shunting arousal to every inch of her body.

Her eyelids lowered, screening her eyes, her lips moving against Ryan's. The man could kiss, and she appreciated his lack of haste. Somehow, most of their clothes disappeared, hitting the floor one by one.

"I can't wait to taste your beautiful pink nipples. I intend to suck one deep into my mouth and play it with my tongue until it's hard and needy," Ryan said.

"And I will suck on the other one so you experience every sensation twofold."

It was amazing how she could tell one man from the other already. Caleb's voice was a touch deeper. Both were sexy, but of the two, Ryan had the edge. She'd always had a thing for men with dark hair. That it came with sexy blue eyes was a real bonus.

"Do you enjoy touching yourself?" The soft question was whispered in her ear and her eyes shot open. She found one man on either side of her. They moved well for big men. She hadn't heard a thing.

"Of course. I know what I like."

"Yet tonight you're letting us touch you." Ryan reached out, letting his hand hover over her breast. It was so close all she needed to do was take a deep breath and he'd graze her nipple.

"Variety is good." Huskiness coated her voice, told of her arousal.

"Most women want to settle down and have a family." Caleb's words held a question, yet she didn't feel as if he were judging her.

"I haven't found a man who engages my interest." Julia shrugged her shoulders hard enough for her breasts to bounce. *Ah, contact.*

Twin grins bloomed. Caleb and Ryan worked in tandem, playing with her breasts, plucking and tweaking.

Pinching. Stroking. Driving her to distraction while she tried to concentrate on the questions they asked.

"So you don't believe in divorce?" Ryan asked.

Julia huffed out a laugh that ended on a needy groan. "This is the weirdest conversation I've ever had during a one-night stand."

"We're not your average men," Caleb said.

Ryan didn't answer. Instead he bent and brushed a soft kiss over her mouth before leaning lower still. He closed his lips around a nipple, the intense heat of his mouth making her moan her pleasure out loud.

"Is he doing it right, sweetheart?" Caleb cupped one arse cheek with his big hand before he, too, claimed a kiss. He was rougher than Ryan, a darker flavor. Different but still fantastic. They kissed her, applying suction together, the sensations making her knees weaken, her folds wetter, plunging her into neediness.

Caleb wrapped an arm around her shoulders, holding her upright with his strength. "Bedroom."

Seconds later, she bounced on the mattress, catching the hungry expressions on their faces. Two tom cats eyeing a mouse. "You're looking at me as if I'm dinner."

Ryan's hands went to the button fly on his jeans, and she tracked the move, noting the bulge at his groin. He paused, and met her gaze, his pale blue eyes glittering with amusement. "You say that as if it's a bad thing."

"Let me see the goods," she said, gesturing with her right

hand.

Ryan watched her from under heavy lids. "I want to remember you like this, all mussed and sexy. That challenge curving your lips. Your beautiful breasts marked by our mouths."

Ryan peeled off his jeans and boxer-briefs together, letting his erection spring out, diverting her attention.

"Nice," she whispered.

Ryan dropped onto the mattress at her side, the warmth of his body sending her pulse leaping to heady heights. His cock dug into her leg, large and hard and oh, so tempting.

"Your turn," she ordered Caleb.

This was a gift. These two men were good and decent. Not once since her arrival at their flat had she felt sleazy or threatened.

Caleb scrambled from his remaining clothes and joined them on the bed, taking the other side so she was sandwiched in the middle. She rubbed against them both, subtly teasing while her hands wandered. She tested golden masculine flesh with her mouth, her teeth, her fingertips.

Ryan stroked her rib cage, tongued the tiny sparkling belly ring at her navel. Her hips arched upward in silent invitation. Luckily Ryan was no dummy and read her hint. While Caleb kissed her mouth and played with her breasts, Ryan went south. Desire tightened her stomach, hummed through her insistently, no longer a low-level pulse.

"Yes," she whispered, quivering because she was so desperate for a greater intimacy. "I need...I need your fingers, your tongue." She could smell her arousal, the scent intertwined with the men's heady musk and the faint trace of soap.

Ryan roughly parted her legs to stare at her. "Aw, beautiful. Caleb, you have to see this. She's swollen and wet. So pretty." Ryan's voice was thick, gritty.

"Because I want you," she muttered. "You're both gorgeous and seem to understand what you're doing." Heat gathered in her cheeks, unusual because she didn't blush.

"Are we embarrassing you?" Ryan winked at Caleb and the heat in her face intensified.

"Are you going to do something instead of staring holes in me?"

"She wants us to do something," Ryan said to Caleb. With a gentle forefinger, he parted her folds while Caleb watched with close attention. Ryan swirled his finger and lifted it to his mouth. Helplessly, she watched him lick it clean. A corresponding twinge of her clit pulled a frustrated moan from her.

"Sweetheart, you're beautiful. Every part of you." Caleb touched her too, running a finger through her juices and raising it to his mouth to taste.

Julia bit her bottom lip, her muscles straining as she rolled her hips upward in silent entreaty. One touch and they'd push her over the edge. She shivered as Ryan sprawled on the mattress again and froze as his warm breath puffed over her inner thighs.

God, so good. Just a little higher.

"Come up here," she said to Caleb. "Let me touch you." She needed something to do, some way to mute this weird urge to beg. She never begged a man for anything. *Never*. Lessons learned from a past boyfriend. Her gaze slid to Caleb's cock, in case her meaning wasn't clear.

Ryan's breath misted across her folds, hit her clit. She let out a throaty moan. A pity this was a one-time thing. They were good. Better than good.

His tongue dipped in for a taste, and it was like a torch to her sexual appetite. The familiar tingles started. Her breath caught as Caleb positioned his body near her head. Ryan tongued around her clit, delicately tasting her flesh and setting fire to her pleasure. He used both his fingers and tongue and she caught her breath, instantly shoved to the precipice. The tingles intensified, growing bigger and more urgent.

They would spoil her for other men. She groped her mind for the why of it all, but couldn't concentrate, not with these wild, frenzied feelings coursing through her body.

"Have you had anal sex before?" Caleb whispered.

"Hmm." She focused on the gathering maelstrom. Blindly, she opened her mouth and closed her lips around

Caleb's cock. She licked, letting his musky flavor flow across her taste buds. She sucked lightly, trying not to move too much because she wanted to ride this rollercoaster, flowing with each curve, each dip and plunge.

"God, Julia. Yeah, just like that," Caleb said. "Not too much. Just enough to tease me."

"Good *hmm* or bad *hmm*?" Ryan asked.

Julia released the head of Caleb's cock. "Depends on the man."

"Is that a challenge?" Ryan watched her tongue flicker out to collect a bead of pre-come from Caleb's slit. Her mouth opened and her cheeks hollowed, sucking Caleb deep. Ryan cursed and she laughed around a mouthful of cock.

Julia was aware of Ryan moving then. A drawer opened and soon a cool wash of lube made her yelp. He tongued around her clit again, keeping her on edge, but backing away whenever he sensed she was getting close. His fingers glided across her puckered entrance. She tensed at first, but Ryan knew what to do. He took it slowly, pushing against the delicate nerves, brushing his fingers back and forth until she relaxed. His finger slipped inside, working in tandem with his tongue brushing her clit. She trembled, but he didn't back off. He caught her throbbing nub between his lips, tortured her while his finger breached her arse.

"That's it, babe." Julia was aware of Caleb murmuring praise and doing his bit to both reassure and drive her desire higher. He plucked at her breasts, his tugs on the hard side, the spurts of pain counteracting nicely with the building pleasure.

Gradually, Ryan added another finger, sinking it into her heat, letting her adjust to the intrusion, twisting his fingers and stimulating her clit. Her hips jerked frantically upward, burying his face in her sex. He sucked on her clit again.

"What are you doing down there, man? She likes it."

And she did. She gripped Ryan's shoulders, the tension in her thighs threatening to crush him, groaning when he pulled away to roll on a condom.

He clasped her hips and lifted her over him. She did her part, grinning as she guided his cock to her entrance. Ryan groaned when she impaled herself, the stretch of his cock perfect. Caleb moved behind her and worked into her gradually until they all writhed in easy strokes.

Her breath caught. So, so good.

Ryan pushed his hand between their sweaty bodies and stroked her clit. She was slippery. Wet and swollen. Unhurried, he caressed her clit with easy glides of his finger.

She shuddered, a spasm tightening her flesh. Her vagina twitched, gripping Ryan's cock and starting a chain reaction. Caleb grunted at the tight squeeze, his stroking becoming erratic, but it didn't matter. She climbed higher, faster, the tingles foretelling climax becoming prickly. Insistent. She strained for pleasure, but held between the two of them she remained trapped, couldn't adjust her hips to get the right pressure. They were teasing her, pushing her, driving her crazy.

"Ryan." She moaned, the tortuous flares of pleasure not enough to propel her into orgasm. More.

More!

SHE TWISTED HER BODY, giving an abrupt jerk. Her breath whooshed out. Her eyes flew open. Confusion gripped her, her clit giving a quick twang before she groaned in frustration.

"Oh hell." She lifted her sweaty face from her page of bullet points, scrubbed her hand over her cheek and a smear of ink came away on her fingertips.

Every muscle in her body ached from falling asleep in the awkward position.

"Hell." The muttered curse squeezed past her lips, and she stumbled into her kitchenette to grab a glass of water, her body still protesting being ripped so violently from the midst of an erotic dream.

She pulled a glass from a cupboard and took the opportunity to splash her face with cool water. Her nipples, swollen and needy, rubbed against her lacy bra while moistness coated the crotch of her panties. She sipped the water, trying to ignore the insistent twinge of arousal.

Muttering another curse, she set the glass on the counter and stomped to her bedroom. She stripped off her clothes, leaving them where they fell. The cool air kissed her skin, made her nipples prickle. Her stomach twisted, arousal a sharp knife cutting at her flesh. With a low groan she sank onto the bed, ripped open the bedside drawer and grabbed her favorite vibe. She shoved it roughly into her pussy, guided the tickler to her clit and turned it on. The low hum pushed up the tension inside her, twisted her gut. Tears welled, dripped down her cheeks even as she exploded into an orgasm that shot white light across the inside of her closed eyes.

Ryan was back. He said he wanted her, and she, weak-willed woman that she was had agreed to let him see her, to help at the club. This was bad. Terrible, and it couldn't end well.

Chapter Six

A KNOCK ON THE front door of Julia's apartment the next morning brought a frown. The clock on the microwave showed it was ten minutes past seven. Heck, she hadn't even started the coffeemaker yet.

She stumbled to the door, yawning. Years of living alone made her check the security hole. She muttered a naughty word and flung the door open.

"What are you doing here?"

Ryan grinned and pressed a quick kiss on her cheek before brushing past her, several brown paper bags and a coffee cup holder in his hands. The scent of brewed coffee trailed after him, an incentive for her not to stomp her foot and kick him out. He'd gone to a lot of trouble and must have sweet-talked someone to let him into the apartment complex.

Julia scurried after him. "And I repeat, what are you

doing here? We were meeting at the café on K' Road."

"I wanted privacy and decided to grab breakfast. I bought your favorite apricot pastries."

"I thought your memory wasn't good." Suspicion colored her tone—she could hear it, and she was certainly thinking he was playing her.

"It's not perfect, but in this case I asked Caleb. He told me you picked an apricot Danish one time we'd breakfasted together."

"I see." But that wasn't the truth. She didn't *see* at all. Ryan confused her, pushed her back into uneasiness. The hours away from him had bolstered her determination. She didn't want to do the long-distance romance, and since Ryan was in the music business, she couldn't see any alternatives. But the moment she was with him, every feminine hormone snapped to attention with a lusty salute, her body melted, and she turned gooey like chocolate in the midday sun.

Danger, Julia Maxwell.

"Latte with low-fat milk." He shunted one coffee across the counter to her. "No sugar. Is that right?"

She gave a clipped nod. "Thank you." It would be petty not to drink the coffee when he'd gone to this trouble. And of course, she needed caffeine to clear the muddiness of her thoughts.

"Should I take a seat?"

Her brows winged upward. "You mean you'll leave if I

ask you to?"

A flash of white teeth gave her an answer. "A meal is always better with company." He ripped open the brown paper bags. "Plates?"

"In the cupboard to your right." She sank onto one of the bar stools at her breakfast counter and watched him. His slow, deliberate actions differed from all those months ago after they'd married. It was almost as if he were concentrating hard, in case he forgot a step.

"How much of your memory is missing?"

"There are still gaps." He hesitated. "I remembered little about us, but some things came back when I saw you at the club. I've been getting new flashes all the time. Tell me about how we decided to get married."

She hesitated, not wanting to relive the heady sweetness of their courtship. The memories made her feel vulnerable. Stupid.

"Please," he said. "The holes are frustrating."

Julia picked up her coffee and took a quick sip. Then, unable to resist his plea, she started talking, "You asked me for my phone number before I left you and Caleb after we spent the night together. You said you wanted to call me when you returned to Auckland."

"Did I call you?"

"You rang me every night until you made it back."

He nodded, his eyes twinkling as he absorbed the details. "That was an intelligent decision. Did we have phone sex?"

She caught her bottom lip between her teeth and stared at the plastic lid of her coffee.

"We did." Masculine smugness floated in the air.

"We might have. Do you want to hear this or not?"

He made a buttoning motion across his lips, his gaze expectant and unnerving.

"When you made it back to Auckland, we spent every hour together. And when you were away, you rang me." The bones of their story without a mention of the way she'd suffered while waiting for his calls—the anticipation and the excitement. The evolving of their relationship from lovers to more. The heady sensation of falling in love.

"When did I tell you about the band?"

"You had a week off over Anniversary weekend and asked me to go to Fiji with you. I agreed, and you sang me one of your songs. You told me about the band and the reasons you'd kept it quiet. You told me you didn't want secrets between us and wanted me to know because I was important to you."

"Was I romantic?" His cocky grin made her want to laugh in response. She took another sip of her coffee instead. "We married in Fiji, didn't we?"

Julia pictured the scene, the warmth of the sun and the sand between her bare toes. She remembered his hands tightening around hers as the marriage celebrant pronounced them man and wife. Their first kiss as a married couple and... "Yes. You remember that?"

"Bits and pieces. All I know is when I look at you I can't sign the divorce papers and walk away. I want us to get to learn about each other again. Sweetheart, I want this marriage. Your face, it was the only thing that kept me going. Memories of you helped me keep sane and balanced through the rest of the tour."

She accepted the plate he handed her and bit into the apricot and custard pastry while she considered his words. The pastry was crisp, the apricot sweet yet tart and the custard oozed into her mouth. She almost moaned at the first bite. Pure sinful delight.

"God, don't do that," he muttered, ripping his gaze off her to stare down at the coffee cupped in his hands.

"Don't do what?"

"Watching you eat reminds me of sex. Do you know how long it's been for me? Do you want me to have an embarrassing accident?"

Julia snorted. "Please. If you're talking about dry spells, I've almost worn out my vibrator."

"Well," he said after a long pause in which she cursed inwardly for giving him the truth. "We could always take care of our problem together."

"Good try. I don't want—"

"Give me a chance to woo you again." He spoke at the same time, causing her to break off her outright rejection. "Please, Julia. You loved me enough to marry me. You owe me this chance to put things right."

"Maybe I don't want to make things right," she whispered. *Liar, liar, pants on fire.* If she didn't want him then why had she rejected every request for a date she'd received in the last few months? She'd stayed at home instead of going out, unless it was with one of the Tight Five. But he'd broken her heart, broken something inside her. If she took a leap, trusted him again...

"You don't mean that."

His grimace and slight shake of his head made her heart twist with indecision of her own. He was right. They might have had a short courtship, but she hadn't gone into their marriage lightly. "Could we shelve the talk of marriage and take each day as it comes instead of planning for the future?" *Please let him say yes.* This was the only way she'd get through the next few months with the club and her mother.

"As long as this is the final discussion we have about divorce, I'm willing to take each day as it comes. Let me help and be a part of this. Let the band rehearse at your club and let me hang out with you. You agreed last night. What's changed?"

Julia dabbed the crumbs on her plate with her finger, unable to meet his gaze. "Everything kept going around in my mind. I didn't sleep much."

"I have a solution for that as well. Let me move in here with you. No," he said when she stood. "I'll sleep in the spare room or on the couch. I don't care. I promise I won't do anything to upset you. We began our marriage with the wrong mindset. We need to start from scratch and learn about each other instead of leaping into bed at the first opportunity."

Julia picked up her pastry and took another mouthful. It tasted even better than the first bite. She swallowed and licked a bit of custard off her top lip before glancing at him again. "I don't—God, don't look at me like that."

He advanced on her then, prowling around the edge of the counter to take her pastry and set it aside. "I won't do anything more than kissing." His warm hand smoothed down her back to come to rest on the curve of one buttock. He pinched hard enough to make her jump, chuckling at her start of surprise. "And some groping. Nothing else until you say we can take things further."

She pushed him away and snatched up her pastry, determined to enjoy the last bite. *Delicious and worth every calorie.* "I—"

"Julia, say yes." He backed her against the counter, until the hard edge dug into her back. His wiry strength held her in place, yet she wasn't threatened.

"You've lost weight," she blurted.

"My appetite disappeared after the mugging, and I haven't been sleeping well. I have headaches." He shuddered but didn't add more.

Most guys would whine but he was straightforward. Smart move on his part. *Yikes, bitch alert.* "How bad are they?"

"They're worse when I get overtired or stressed."

"What did the doctors say?"

"They told me the headaches will taper off. So, do you feel sorry enough for me to invite me to stay?"

"You're playing me." Bother, she couldn't keep her bitchy side contained.

"A little." A cheeky grin surfaced—one containing an edge of flirtation and a smidgeon of boyish charm. The sort of grin that tugged at a person and made them want to return the sentiment. His dark eyelashes fluttered, a striking frame around his pale blue eyes. "Is it working?"

Julia bit her lip to stop laughing, ultra-aware of the gleam in his eyes, the light press of his weight against her and the prod of his erection. To give him credit, he didn't grind against her or do anything else tacky. Instead they stared at each other, silent messages flying back and forth while she tried to remain grounded.

"I'm going to kiss you." A clear statement of intent.

She sucked in a harsh breath. She would tell him to move away so she could finish her coffee. Yes, she'd do that any second now. His head lowered, coming closer. The scent of soap, herby with a touch of lemon, filled her next breath. Then his lips were on hers and he was kissing her. His mouth was gentle but insistent too. Immediately he shoved her into the past, into a dreamlike state where pleasure danced through her senses, prickled in the damp heat between her legs. She moaned and clutched his shoulders, bringing his weight against her. So good. She could kiss him all day, exist in this world of desire and the beginnings of erotic pleasure. A world without problems.

As if he read her jumble of thoughts, he pulled back, his mouth reddened, his lips slightly wet from their kiss. The sense of loss was unbearable. She leaned into him, silently imploring him for more.

"Julia, your phone is going."

"Huh?"

He turned away and grabbed her cell phone off the countertop. She accepted it from him and took two tottering steps back, groping her foggy mind for sanity. A trembling finger stabbed the right button to answer the call. "Y-yes?"

"Julia," he whispered.

She couldn't look at him, not even when he repeated her name. Her coffee appeared in front of her nose, and she realized that was what he was trying to tell her. She clutched the cardboard cup and tried to ignore her unsteady hand.

"Are you there?" Maggie's familiar voice dispersed some of the mist inside her head.

"Sorry. Just a bit distracted." She glared at Ryan when he snorted.

"Do you want to share a cab to the club with us?"

"I thought I'd jump on the loop bus. It goes right past

the club."

"Good idea. We'll do the same. Be there in five minutes."

"No, I'm not dressed yet. I-I slept in." Julia closed her eyes, but pretending she wasn't in her kitchen and standing a short distance from Ryan didn't lessen the agitated thump of her heart. "I'll need another ten minutes at least."

"Okay, we'll meet you at the café," Maggie said. "See you later."

"You didn't tell her I was here."

"That will be obvious when we walk into the café together and both say we've had breakfast already," Julia shot back. "Where's Caleb?"

"Probably panicking because he can't find me. He's turned into a fusspot since my accident. I should ring him before he leaves for Tauranga. He's visiting his parents for a few days."

"He's your friend," Julia said. "Friends can mother you when you need it. Why aren't you going home too?"

His gaze narrowed on her. "Caleb is my friend, and that's all he'll ever be to you."

Suddenly the tension between them was a tight spring ready to uncoil. "I was talking about my friends, but since you've brought up the subject, we discussed our *ménage à trois* when we first talked about marriage."

Ryan's breath hissed out. He scrubbed a hand over his face before he looked at her again. "I have no recollection of the conversation."

He seemed lost, and his expression made her want to wrap her arms around him in a comforting hug. She quashed the idea to maintain a grip on her sanity.

"What did—" His voice cracked, and he gave a whip-sharp cough before he continued. "What did we decide?"

"That Caleb was our friend and we didn't need a third person in our bed."

"Thank you," he mumbled.

Julia squeezed his arm and moved away when sympathy urged her to do more. "I'd better shower. My list is on the counter. Why don't you take a look and tell me if anything jumps out at you?"

She swallowed the remains of her cooling coffee. "Won't be long." Julia hurried to the bathroom, telling herself she was making a huge mistake. She should sprint in the opposite direction, or at the very least, approach her lawyer about a restraining order. But no, she intended to invite him to stay. One way or another they'd use the proximity to discover if their marriage should continue.

The promised ten minutes later, she sauntered into the kitchen. Ryan was on the phone.

"Julia and I needed to talk," he said into the phone. "We intend to catch the loop bus to meet the others at the café near the club before we start work. Yeah. Say hello to your parents for me. I'll see you on Monday afternoon."

On seeing her, he disconnected the call, his gaze taking in her tight blue jeans and her favorite black tunic top that made the most of her curves. She hadn't bothered with much makeup—just a swish of mineral powder and a clear lip gloss. Her hair was in a high ponytail, imminently practical for work.

"You look beautiful."

"Thanks." His compliment brought a rush of pleasure because the heated glow in his eyes told her it was genuine.

"You can move in," she said before she could rethink her decision. "There's a spare bedroom. I want to take things slow." She intended to work long hours anyway. She wouldn't spend much of the next two weeks at her apartment.

"You won't regret it." Ryan wanted to shout out in exhilaration but held himself in check. This was his last chance—his only chance—and he didn't want to blow it. Nerves simmered in the pit of his stomach, much the same as the ones he experienced seconds before walking on stage for a gig. She'd given him an opening, and it was up to him to make sure his plan succeeded.

They walked into the café together almost half an hour later. Julia paused in the doorway, scanning the interior until she found her friends.

"Do you want another coffee and something to eat?"

A baby cried at a nearby table, and Julia winced, looking

away with a moue of distaste. Normally he liked kids, but the unhappy cries pushed the tingles of a beginning headache into low gear. "Julia?" he prompted.

"Another latte and two sandwiches to take away," she said, lifting a hand to wave at her friends. "It looks as if they're nearly finished. They won't want to wait for us." She turned away before looking back at him. "Make sure you get something to eat. Something fattening. You can't afford to lose any more weight."

The baby stopped crying, and Julia sent a quick glance in that direction. The tension that slid from her shoulders echoed in the reactions of the people sitting at the next table.

"Coffee and sandwiches it is." Ryan grinned and headed for the counter. She'd paid attention to him and cared enough to worry about his health. He spied Caleb arriving and tilted his chin in recognition.

Caleb joined him as Ryan perused the selection of food. "What are you smirking about?"

Ryan knuckle-bumped with his friend, delight at his wife's concern still tickling him. "Julia is worried about my weight loss. What are you doing here?"

"I thought you might want your guitar and music before I left." Caleb checked to see if anyone might overhear him. "I told you she sneaks glances at you when she thinks you won't notice. Was she okay about you turning up this morning?"

"She's letting me move into the apartment with her."

"Way to go!" Another knuckle-bump ensued.

"I'm in the spare bedroom," Ryan said. "But it's a start."

"Good going. Are you working on our arrangements this morning?"

"Yes. I didn't get around to asking Julia how much she wants to charge us for rehearsal space."

"We can help her with some of her renovation work. I wonder if she'll let me help with hiring the dancers."

Ryan let out a snort. "Good luck with that."

With coffee and sandwiches in hand, he and Caleb wandered over to the table of friends. It was almost like hanging out with the band given the energy pulsing through the air and the sense of solidarity. The positive vibe was addictive, and for the first time in months, Ryan experienced normal and grounded instead of drifting outside himself. Obviously his heart had known something—someone—was missing even if his brain remained clueless.

"Caleb brought my guitar and music before he heads off to Tauranga." Ryan edged around the table so he stood by Julia. *Sick puppy*. But now he'd found her again, he was only comfortable when he was near her. No doubt a psychologist would have a ball dissecting the confidence.

"I'm finished." Susan pushed her partially eaten plate away. "I can't eat all this if I want to look good for the reality show."

"You'll need the energy," Julia said. "I intend to work you hard and crack the whip if you slacken. And then I'll start the dance training. You said you wanted to learn, right?"

And work them, she did.

Exhaustion dogged Ryan's steps during the late afternoon. He and Julia's friend, Connor, had spent most of the day preparing the walls for painting, perched on ladders and removing the heavy velvet curtains.

"That's the last one." Connor dropped the red velvet, and it crashed to the ground with a huge cloud of dust. He sneezed before climbing down the ladder.

Ryan scanned the walls. Although years of smoke had discolored the white paint, the curtains had shielded the surfaces too. "A good scrub might be enough," he said. "The paint isn't peeling off anywhere."

"I agree," Connor said. "It's not the big job I envisaged."

"That looks better," Julia said, coming up behind him.

"What color are you painting it?" Connor asked.

Julia halted beside them, and once again the sense of rightness filled Ryan. "Christina suggested a deep midnight blue with borders of gold as accents. What do you think?"

"Sounds good," Ryan said. "A dark color might allow you to project images onto the walls too."

Julia seized his arm and squeezed, her eyes blazing with enthusiasm. "Great idea. I've been trying to work out how to make our acts and the club different and unique."

"Good enough for a kiss?" He tapped a spot on his cheek, his breath hitching when he saw her hesitate. He'd done this to her, made her cautious. She wavered for so long the silence became uncomfortable.

Then she threw her arms around his neck and kissed him on the mouth. *Whoa!* Zero to a hundred in seconds flat. Urgency thrummed through him, his hands gripping her shoulders in case she pulled away. He took the kiss deeper, drinking her up like a thirsty man, savoring her heat and the press of her breasts against his chest, storing every single second to pull out later when he was alone.

"The girls have arrived for the auditions." Maggie spoke loudly, right next to his ear. He started, pulled to the present and slackened his hold but didn't release Julia.

"Oh, good." Maggie wrinkled her nose. "I thought I'd need a hose to separate the pair of you. Didn't you hear me the first time? Only three dancers turned up from the agency. We don't want them to get the wrong idea."

"Thank you, Maggie," Julia said.

Ryan winked at Julia, and she grinned back. Relief was a swift kick in the guts. His manhandling hadn't scared her.

"I'd better check out these dancers," she said. "Take a break or finish up for the day." She strode away, and Ryan stared after her.

"You've got it bad for her," Connor said.

"Yeah." No denying the truth.

"If you hurt her, you'll have me to deal with." Connor's hard gaze backed up his statement. "She—" He broke off, chagrin chasing across his face.

"What?"

"Under her tough exterior, she's fragile. You want a drink or something to eat? I'm going for some fresh air."

But he wasn't inviting Ryan along. "I'm fine." And because he wasn't satisfied with the way the conversation had gone, he added, "I have no intention of hurting Julia."

Connor held his gaze for a long second. "Make sure you don't."

A SONG WITH A good strong beat swelled through the air. The first woman started her routine, and it took Julia two minutes to decide she wouldn't do. Julia held up her hand, a signal to Christina to stop the music.

"Where did you say you'd worked before?" Julia asked.

"The Purple Pussy."

Julia tapped her pen against her notepaper. "If I take you on, you must learn some new routines and attend training classes."

"I can do a strip routine."

Julia didn't intend to argue. "Thank you. I've seen enough."

The woman stomped away muttering under her breath.

The second and third women, both in their early twenties and dark-haired, performed their routines, the unoriginal, lackluster moves shoving Julia's spirits even lower. She signaled for the music to stop and strode up on the stage. "Are you both willing to do training?"

"That would be great," the first said.

The second woman nodded. "I haven't been dancing long. I love to learn new routines."

"Excellent," Julia said crisply. "We might as well start now."

She strode up onto the stage and stood in front of a pole. "Start the music please, Christina."

"Wait for us," Maggie said, coming running. Susan followed swiftly behind and they took their places in front of a pole. Christina started the music and joined them. Julia took them through a grueling training session, starting with the basics just as her mother had shown her.

Finally, she took them through a cool-down and strode over to stop the music.

"Next time I'm bringing my workout gear," Maggie said. "That was harder than the gym sessions Connor designed for me."

"You'll need a pair of heels too. Black if possible, so you get used to dancing in shoes rather than flats," Julia said. "Guys love a woman's legs in heels."

"I'll vouch for that," Ryan said.

Julia blew out a breath. "I didn't realize you were still

here."

"Wouldn't have missed it," he said. "Great job. You girls are quick learners."

"We have a way to go yet." Julia turned to speak to her new employees. She didn't seem to have put them off. "Can you both make it here around two tomorrow afternoon?"

They assured her they could and left.

"I won't be able to move tomorrow," Susan said. "My muscles are seizing up."

"Take a hot bath when you get home," Julia said. "I want you fighting fit tomorrow at nine."

Her friends left for the day, leaving her alone with Ryan.

"What do you think?" she asked. "Is this fixable?" Although she'd hated working here and living above the club as a child, this time seemed different. The club was part of her family history, and she was the last of the Maxwell line. She owed it to her mother and the other family members who had worked to keep the place alive, despite the obstacles.

"As long as you can get the right staff," Ryan said.

She nodded, glad he wasn't offering platitudes. "That will be the hardest part. None of those dancers were up to the standards Mum set when I worked here."

"We'll do it."

"I thought you needed to work on your music. You did stuff for me all day."

"I wrote a lot of music during the tour. While the others partied, I spent hours writing new material."

"What about the photos on the Internet?"

"I attended some of the after concert parties, the ones I couldn't get out of. You must know how the paparazzi operate. They pay women to drape themselves around us, and try to take off the masks we use when we do publicity. I try to discourage the touchy-feely stuff, but it doesn't always work."

A flash of the last photo she'd seen blasted to the forefront of her mind. The lip lock. Ryan's hands gripping the woman's shoulders and drawing her closer. A shudder ran through her, and she tried to force the image away. It refused to shift, hovering like the smell of a putrid egg.

It wasn't Ryan's fault he'd come last in the line of rotten bad boys. It wasn't fair to cast him in the same group as the others who'd kicked her down when it suited them. Cheated, lied and given her an STD. Her mind froze at the last thought, jagged pain hacking at her psyche.

"We always attend those parties in full disguise, using our masks instead of our stage makeup. How do you know it was me?"

She puffed out a hard breath, struggled to regain her equilibrium. "Please. You think I can't recognize my husband when I see him?"

A little of the devil shone in his eyes again. "Good to hear."

"Besides, you all have your initials on the masks. I saw the D."

"Oh." The teasing left him, a trace of frustration coming to the surface. "The photo might have been manipulated or taken out of context. Some of the women test our boundaries."

"You think?" Oh, he was quick. She turned away, unable to watch his expression. He said he hadn't done it on purpose while she'd decided the suggestive photo was a sign he wanted out of their marriage.

He said nothing of an accusatory nature, yet her lack of trust must have cut deep. An apology—it wouldn't be enough. "I'm sorry. It was hard to hold onto trust when you were incommunicado. When you're alone your mind twists everything."

"Don't. Don't, sweetheart." He marched to her, pulling her into the circle of his arms. She pressed her cheek against his chest, the ache in her chest so painful she wanted to cry out. She'd gone into her marriage with the intention of forever. But this—this showed her how little she'd invested in their marriage, how easily she'd given up on her husband.

"It's all right," Ryan murmured.

She lifted her head to stare at him. "How can it be?"

"We have a second chance," he said. "Most people don't get this opportunity, and we shouldn't waste it."

CHAPTER SEVEN

A NEW TENSION SLITHERED through Julia's veins now. Ten at night, and she and Ryan had arrived back at her apartment a few minutes ago. They'd stopped at the flat Ryan and Caleb shared for Ryan to pick up some of his gear. Now that the door closed behind them, her apartment seemed too intimate. Ryan's scent ghosted around her, enticing and seductive. He took up space, the air in her kitchen.

"I'm knackered," he said, holding his hands in the small of his back and leaning back. "I swear the painting prep was more exhausting than anything I've done this year."

"You've used different muscles. Have a hot bath while I clear the spare room for you. The bathroom is down the passage on the right."

"No, I'll help."

"Go and have a bath." Sharp and terse. She bit her lip

at the appearance of *Bitch Julia*. Consciously lowering her voice, she tried again. "If you use the bathroom first, then I can jump into the shower straight away."

He nodded, his sexy lips perking up into the beginnings of a smile. "You've seen me naked before."

"Bathroom." The sudden need to laugh tugged at her, and she pointed. "Go." To her relief, he left and she waited until his footsteps faded before she sagged against the kitchen counter. She didn't understand how he did it. Yesterday morning she'd been so certain she wanted a divorce. Ryan was muddying her thoughts, confusing her. Now she didn't know what she wanted, what to do for the best. He'd sounded sincere about the photos—she didn't sense he was lying.

With a sigh, she strode down the passage, grabbed clean linen, and continued to her spare bedroom. He was splashing around in the water already, his husky voice singing a classic Jackson song. She smiled before she could stop herself. Heck, why didn't she admit the truth? In two days he'd charmed her all over again. She didn't stand a chance.

Julia finished making the bed for Ryan and cleared away some of the surface clutter that had encroached into her guest room. Once she was satisfied, she wandered to her own room, collected her robe and paused. She sank onto her bed. No, as weak as she was feeling now, it wasn't a good idea to walk into the bathroom and jump into the shower with Ryan still lolling about in the bath.

So she sat there, waiting and trying not to imagine the beads of water covering his chest, trying not to listen to the husky ballad he was singing—something she hadn't heard before but one that echoed the need stirring inside her now. The singing coming from the bathroom trailed off.

She froze, sucking in a breath when she heard the water gurgle down the drain. Then her imagination turned redcoat. A vision of his broad shoulders filled her mind as she conjured details from the past. His trim waist and hips. His sexy tattoo. His muscles flexing with each rub of the towel along his limbs. One of her towels. A low-level buzz bloomed in her sex. A pithy curse escaped, and she leaped to her feet. The movement made her conscious of the way her clothes clung to her skin, the lace of her bra abrasive against her nipples.

"Julia, I'm done."

"Thank you." A boon to her sanity. "The room is ready for you." She opened her door and came face-to-face with him. Her steps faltered. "Good night, Ryan. Thanks for helping me today."

"Goodnight, Julia." He entered the spare bedroom and closed the door behind him, leaving her standing in the passage, gaping at the wooden barrier between them.

Well, what had she expected?

Yanking from her reverie, she stalked into the bathroom

and shut the door. The room was steamy after Ryan's use, and those ridiculous visions ran through her mind again, springing into sharp relief.

"Fuck." She cursed again because it felt good on her tongue. Her mother would scold her for the bad language. Susan would for certain, if she'd been present. Julia stripped off her clothes and jumped under the water. It was only lukewarm and should have dampened the desire streaking through her veins. But the temperature heated all too quickly.

"Heck," she muttered.

She grabbed her scented gel and applied it with rough, scrubbing motions of her shower buddy. Maybe she could rub out her desire. Didn't happen. On completing the brisk wash, every inch of her skin tingled. She shut the water off and toweled dry. In her bedroom, she smoothed chocolate body butter on her limbs.

Her body revved up again, her skin prickling all over. Damn it all. She slapped on the last of the lotion, switched off the light and jumped into bed. This fantasizing—it had to stop. It wasn't smart, even if it was grown-up!

Julia closed her eyes and willed herself to sleep.

A shout woke her. High and terrified, it seemed to hang in the air. Her heart raced and a ripple of goose flesh rose on her arms and legs. She half sat, unsure if she'd had a bad dream or if it was something else.

Another low cry sounded, and she jumped off the bed.

She switched on her light and was through the door, standing before the doorway of her spare room in seconds flat. A third cry propelled her forward. She opened the door and rushed to the bed. The light from her room allowed her to make out his form. Ryan was still asleep, but he was twisting and turning, moaning in the throes of a dream.

"Ryan, wake up. Ryan." Gingerly, she reached for his arm. "Ryan."

His eyes snapped open, wide and unfocused. "Julia?"

"Yes, you were shouting. A bad dream?"

"Yeah." He sat up with a grunt and swiped his hand across his face. "Thanks. I'm sorry I woke you."

Julia stood, trying to keep her gaze off his bare chest, his dragon tattoo. She ignored the urge nipping her heels, the one telling her to slide right into bed with him. "I'll let you get back to sleep." Like a coward, she fled back to her room. She slid beneath the sheets, her mind too busy to rest.

Seconds later, she heard the pad of footsteps.

"Hey, Julia. I can't sleep. I thought I'd make some hot chocolate, if you have some."

"I'll get it for you." She started to get out of bed again.

"No." He stayed her with a stop gesture. "I'll make it." He was gone before she could argue. After debating following him she slumped against her pillow. No, that would be plain silly, and she'd already reached her stupidity quotient today.

She reached for her handbag and retrieved her list. With a pen in hand, she checked through each item and crossed out two.

Ryan appeared in the doorway. "Julia, I made one for you since you're awake too." He handed her a cup, the rich scent of chocolate wafting to her. He'd dropped four marshmallows in the top and they'd already partially melted.

Instead of leaving, he perched on the end of her bed. He was wearing black boxer-briefs and nothing else. The man sure looked good, albeit on the skinny side.

"Don't get cold." Grief, she sounded like a mother. Unfamiliar heat swept into her cheeks, and she focused on her hot chocolate. "There's something wrong with me." The words came out unbidden, and once she'd uttered them, she couldn't take them back.

"Oh? Are you sick?"

She half-laughed. "No, it's you. When I look at you I get inappropriate feelings."

"You say that like it's a bad thing." His brows winged toward his hairline. "Have you turned to religion?"

"No! Not that there's anything wrong with religion. I—you put me off balance. I can't think straight."

His charm came to the fore in a dazzling smile, and she gulped. She had no defenses against him when he applied his flirtation. It reached the point where she couldn't make proper decisions. No, that wasn't quite right. She arrived at conclusions, but her instincts steered her wrong.

"That's not inappropriate," he said. "I enjoy spending time with you."

"But that's the problem," she almost wailed. "We can't be together every day. Because of your job you need to travel overseas. Now that I'm helping Mum with the club, I have even more reason to stay in Auckland. I—what happens if I need you or you need me, and we're in different countries?"

"Other people manage long-distant relationships," Ryan said. "Can I get under the covers? It's getting cold." He pulled back the duvet and slid into her bed before a refusal was born, let alone passed her lips.

She gave an exasperated huff. "Don't mind me." She drank the last of her chocolate and set her cup aside.

"We can work out something," Ryan said.

"Things didn't work for us last time. I don't want to go through that hell again."

Ryan put his cup down and turned to her. "I'm sorry. I understand the last months can't have been easy for you. No one could have predicted I'd get mugged and lose my memory."

Julia struggled to find the right words to explain her inner conflict. "It's not going to be as easy as you say. Seeing photos of you with other women brings back things I'd rather forget. I thought I had a handle on the past, but bad memories keep interfering. It's not fair to you. I know that, but...it just happens."

"But you're willing to try. There's something special between us. You've said you react to my charm."

"I have no idea what to do." A yawn took her by surprise. "I'm tired. I need sleep otherwise I'll never get everything done before we reopen."

"Can I stay here?"

"We're not having sex."

This time he didn't flash a grin in her direction. "I don't want to have another bad dream."

Julia yawned again, too tired to argue. "All right." After he'd settled, she turned off the light. For a while she was overly conscious of his body warmth and held her muscles tense. When he let out a long breath and lay on his side, she turned in the opposite direction and closed her eyes.

The alarm blared at six-thirty, and Julia smacked at it with an uncoordinated hand. The beeps cut off. Supremely warm and comfortable, she didn't want to move.

A hand curled around her hip, and a kiss landed on her bared neck. "I like waking up this way."

Oops, awake now. She did too but wasn't about to admit it. Dangerous territory. "I need to get moving."

"Give me a kiss good morning."

"Morning breath," she muttered.

"Can I feel you up instead?"

She spluttered out a laugh. "No."

"Damn, you're no fun."

Julia sprang out of bed before she weakened. "Do you want coffee?"

"Is the pope Catholic?"

"Why yes. I believe he is."

She pulled on a comfy pair of sweats, and after hesitating, removed her sleep shirt and replaced it with a T-shirt. Out in the kitchen, she made a quick call to check on her mother and started the coffee. The coffeemaker was soon gurgling, and she stopped to wonder if she'd made a mistake in sharing her bed. No, she decided. She'd slept better than she had in months. While she waited for the coffee, she ran through some of her morning stretch routine.

Ryan joined her in the kitchen. Without asking, he wrapped his arms around her from behind, tugging her against his chest.

"I thought we were confining ourselves to friends-only," she said.

"Nope, I never agreed to that. This is wooing, baby. I intend to persuade you to my way of thinking."

"Do you have any suggestions for promo for the club?" Not the smoothest change of subject, but she'd run with it. "I need to complete everything this week and get moving on the advertising."

"Coward."

"I'm in work-mode now," Julia said. "That's got to be

my focus."

His blue eyes narrowed a fraction. "I'm up for the task."

"I don't want you to look on me as a challenge. I have to concentrate on *Maxwell's*."

"Of course you do. I've written a theme song for your club. You could play it when you're introducing dancers or something. Use it as a signal to the audience that something is about to happen."

Julia stared at him, warmth twining through her. "You wrote a song for me?"

"You're my inspiration. Even when your name escaped me, I dreamed about you. Your face and your pretty blonde hair filled my sleep." He ran his fingertips over her cheek.

God, he was so sweet. Unable to think of what to say or to fight her desire any longer, she said, "We'll have sex. Tonight."

Yeah, that would sort out her waffling. A little hot and heavy sex would sort out everything.

"Gotta go," she said, not giving him a chance to answer. "I will be in and out of the club today, plus I have the girls coming to practice dance routines." Finished, she snapped her mouth shut and ran for cover, the weight of his stare following as she disappeared back into her bedroom, her heart spooked into erratic beats. *Well,* she thought on reaching the safety of her bedroom. *Nothing like laying down a challenge.*

"I've booked a hen's party for the week after next," Susan greeted her. "I didn't think you'd mind if I suggested it to my cousin."

"Great!" Julia said. "I guess I should buy a diary to keep track of our bookings."

Maggie dragged herself through the door of the club. Her pained gaze swept their faces before settling to glower at Julia. "Tell me you have stiff muscles too."

Susan's groan was heartfelt. "Thank goodness. I thought it was just me. Julia's not limping one bit, so I was trying to pretend I'm fine. I had to roll out of bed this morning, and I took five minutes to get moving."

Christina walked gingerly through the double doors, wincing with every step, and Julia had trouble restraining her chuckle.

Julia glanced from one friend to the next. "I'm sorry. I didn't think about sore muscles. I still go to dance classes two or three times a week."

"It's not natural, twisting a body into graceful arcs," Maggie grumbled. "I had to get Connor to give me a massage—"

"Don't rub it in," Christina said. "Some of us don't have a handyman."

Susan nodded emphatically. "What she said."

"It will get better," Julia promised.

"We're holding you to that promise," Susan said, her expression glum as she attempted a cautious stretch. "But I'm not sure I believe you."

"Well, she should buy the first round of margaritas when we hit the pub again," Maggie said.

Julia grinned at her three friends, so grateful for their support. "Deal."

Music played—guitar with a faint bluesy tone. A husky voice commenced singing, and Julia froze, memories slipping over her. Good memories, ones of laughter and sensuality. Then the words of the song registered, and her heart did a rapid change up in gear. He'd done this for her.

"Oh, my god," Susan shrieked. "A theme song for the club. It's perfect."

"He's good," Maggie said.

"I agree," Christina said, wincing as she shifted her weight and turned to watch Ryan on the stage. "If the rest of his band is as good as him they won't be roadies for much longer."

Ryan finished his song and everyone broke into applause. Julia swallowed, the emotions booming inside her almost too much to contain.

He stood and bowed from the waist. "Thank you. Thank you very much," he said in a corny Elvis impression.

"Back to work everyone," Julia said, clapping her hands to hurry them along.

"I have suggestions for the costumes," Christina said, producing a sketchbook from the red tote bag in her left hand. "Do you have time to go over them now?"

"Sure. My office? I'll meet you there. I want a quick word with Ryan first," Julia said.

"Clock is ticking," Christina said. "No dilly-dallying with that handsome husband of yours."

"I'm the boss. I can dilly if I want." Two days ago she would have hotly disputed Christina's words. Even yesterday, but the wretched man had worked his magic once again. And then, to top things off, he'd seduced her with a special song. She turned her back on her grinning friend and strode toward the stage.

"What do you think?"

"I loved it. Thank you. Your song is perfect."

"Worth a kiss?" His unrepentant grin had an answering smile tugging at her.

Her nose lifted into the air. "Maybe."

He glanced past her, but Julia didn't need to turn around to tell everyone was watching them. Not when their gazes bored into her back.

"I'll record it for you as soon as Caleb gets back from Tauranga. It should be ready for opening night."

"Thanks," she whispered, and because she couldn't resist, she cupped his upturned face between her hands and kissed him. Gentle and sweet, the physical contact sent longing crawling through her veins. When she pulled back, they stared at each other for a long moment.

"Tonight?" he asked.

"Tonight." Julia turned away because she didn't trust herself not to touch him again. The guitar started as she hurried to her office. It was something new and foot tapping, a tune to entice her to stay to hear the rest of the song. Unfortunately work and responsibility beckoned. She didn't search out her friends, keeping her gaze lowered as if she were concentrating on a weighty problem. A sharp snort escaped her. Heck, she wasn't fooling anyone, least of all her friends. Let the teasing begin.

When she arrived in her mother's office, Christina had removed fabric samples from her tote bag and opened her sketch book.

"Have you hired any new dancers?"

Julia scowled at her friend's opening salvo. "No. Most of the decent ones are working at the club down the road. I talked to my mother earlier. From what she said, we're not likely to find any at present. She's tried everywhere."

"I suspected as much," Christina said. "I might have a way you can work around a staff shortage. Have you decided whether to stick with stripping or are you going to specialize in burlesque?"

"I'm not sure," Julia said. "My mind keeps going back and forth on this. *The Last Frontier* has always been a strip club. It's what the customers expect."

"Except custom has dropped off. This is the perfect time

to change things up. You'll attract more hen's nights if it's burlesque. Go for it and switch to burlesque. It will be a point of difference to your competitors. You'd be targeting a different set of customers."

Julia nodded. Christina's summation, stated so succinctly, helped her decide. She nodded again, more categorically. "You're right. We'll take the burlesque path."

"Good. That will make the costuming easier and challenging too. A suggestion. Your dancers should wear masks. It will make your dancers mysterious and will work to your advantage. Even if you can't hire enough dancers before opening day your existing ones will look different by changing masks and costumes and wearing wigs. The audience will never realize you've only got four or five girls dancing because each set and costume change will make them appear different."

A delighted laugh escaped Julia. "So simple. Yes, that's perfect. I can dance myself if necessary."

"If you agree to the masks, I can dance too—if I'm good enough. I wasn't about to agree to stripping in front of everyone."

"You'd still be stripping off a few layers," Julia warned, touched by her friend's offer.

"But my bare body wouldn't be out there for everyone to see," Christina said. "Believe me, that's not a sight for enticing customers. The idea of the tease and seduction sounds heaps better."

Julia grinned. "Agreed. Show me what you've got for costume ideas."

They spent the next half hour discussing fabrics, fans and feathers with Christina feverishly jotting down notes.

"I can put these costumes together with no trouble," Christina said. "It won't cost much either."

"Come and see what Mum has upstairs in the flat. She has an entire room of costumes. We might be able to use some of the props at least. Most of the stuff is skimpy though."

"I might fit skimpy if I keep up with the amount of exercise I've done during the last couple of days."

Julia led the way up to her mother's flat. "We're here to check out the costumes," she said when they popped in on Elise and Janet.

Elise smiled, but Julia could see her mother forced it. Her pale features told of her poor night of sleep. "You know where they are."

Julia hesitated before deciding to tell her mother of her plans. "I've decided to take the burlesque angle rather than straight stripping. I'm hoping the point of difference will bring in more customers—some new ones who wouldn't have otherwise come to the club."

Elise gave a throaty laugh of surprise. "Did you know that originally we did burlesque rather than stripping? My grandparents probably spun in their graves when my father changed things to attract the customers."

"Then you don't mind?"

"Of course I don't. You have a good head on your shoulders. The business is in your veins after all. Check the suitcases right at the back of the wardrobe. I packed the old costumes in there a few years ago. They might smell of mothballs, but there are some wonderful outfits. They might be just what you're looking for."

Julia kissed her mother's cheek. "Thanks. You try and catch more sleep. Are you still seeing the specialist later?"

"Yes. Janet is taking me."

"Okay." Julia smiled her thanks at Janet. "Just shout if either of you need anything."

Julia and Christina walked into the large room. Costumes hung from freestanding racks, each outfit covered with plastic.

"Where do we start?" Christina asked.

Julia strode over to the wardrobe door, wheeling a rack out of her way to clear her path. She opened the door and pulled out two large suitcases. "These are the ones Mum meant. Can I leave you to it while I take care of stuff downstairs? I intend to have an earlier dance practice today because the painters are coming at three. Connor arranged for most of his rugby team to come and help."

Christina opened the first suitcase and waved her away. "I'll shout if I need you."

The rest of the day passed rapidly. Dance practice worked well and the progress pleased Julia. The guys arrived and soon the place smelled of fresh paint. Three hours later, she stood in the middle of the club and turned slowly, surveying the walls. The midnight blue color was perfect. Excitement did a slow burn inside her stomach. For the second time today goose bumps pebbled her skin—in a good way.

There were still details to arrange, but opening day couldn't come soon enough. Yes, there was some of the Maxwell businessman welling up inside her now.

"Man, I'm beat," Ryan said when they caught the lift to her apartment.

"Me too," Julia said with a yawn. "I feel as if we're making progress though. It's a good sensation. Do you want first shower?"

"Thanks." Ryan took the keys from her and opened the door because she was carrying a load of costumes in plastic wrapping.

"Christina picked out some costumes for the hen's night, and she wanted me to try them on to make sure they fit."

"You're dancing?"

"Yeah." She entered the apartment in front of him. "I'll do a dress parade for you. You can give me your expert opinion."

In her bedroom she stripped down to her underwear and glanced at the first of the costumes. A long black dress with silver embroidery. It was reminiscent of something one of the glamour movie stars of the thirties would have worn. She'd have to lose the bra.

"Ryan, are you there?" She heard him coming and turned her back to the door while holding the bodice in place. "I need help with the zipper."

Warm hands tugged the zip into place then settled on her bare shoulders.

"Wow," he said as he turned her around to face him. "Are all the costumes this elegant?"

"Yes, we're doing a Hollywood glamour theme for the hen's night. Sort of thirtyish era."

"Do you need music?"

"Christina and I thought we'd sort out a soundtrack of music from that era."

"Would you like live music?"

"You'd do that?"

"Yes." His short tone told her he was a little pissed with her for doubting him.

"You haven't been here," she flared defensively. "I'm not used to counting on you."

His face clouded, a hint of pain twisting his lips. "You're right. I'd be honored to provide live music for your first function. I can't promise Caleb's help. He'll have to answer for himself, but I'm in. Will you want me to wear a costume too?"

"I'll discuss it with Christina and we'll come up with something for you. Can you unzip me?" She slid the dress off and reached for the next. The choked sound from Ryan stilled her hands.

"You're beautiful."

Julia picked up the gown—a slinky red—and held it against her. After her stripper years, nudity never worried her, but Ryan's avid gaze roving her body felt different, her skin pulsing under his visual interest. "I didn't think."

"Let me help with the fastener." His voice was lower than usual and rough in a sensual way.

"It zips up the side." Without looking at him, she stepped into the dress and pulled it up over her hips. "Do you like it?"

"I thought these were costumes for strippers?"

"Some are, but Christina and I decided they'd work for me to wear while introducing each act. I'm aiming for sophistication. Do you agree?"

"You're a knockout and your ideas are perfect." His gaze traced the curves of her breasts, cupped and lifted in the tight bodice. In a trick of the light he appeared predatory and when he stalked around her to view the back of the gown, the similarity to a dangerous feline heightened. He settled in a casual sprawl on the bed. "Are there more?"

"Yes." She undid the gown and stepped out of it. The next number was the one Christina had dubbed sexy ringmaster. Black and white, it was more bathing suit in coverage, leaving her legs bare. A tight black jacket completed the outfit.

"You need black boots with spiky heels and fishnet stockings with that one," Ryan said.

Julia nodded, in full agreement after a quick glance in her full-length mirror. "Christina has a good eye for fashion. These fit perfectly. I thought you were going to have a shower."

"And miss the show? Not likely. Besides, you might need my help again."

A snort escaped her.

"I hope you're not going to make that sound on stage," he said. "You'll send the customers running to the opposition."

"Funny man." Julia reached for the blue. It was almost the same color as the paint she'd chosen for the walls of the club. Gold sequins decorated the neckline and hem.

"Beautiful." Ryan's verdict. "You'll need to wear your hair up."

Julia glanced in the mirror, agreeing with his assessment. She pulled on another skimpy bathing suit number in red and black that came with a long matching skirt.

"Perfect," Ryan said, his eyes skimming her body. A hot sensation prickled in the wake of his gaze, edgy heat making her shift her weight from foot to foot. "Come and shower with me."

She took a few seconds to comprehend. An instinctive rebuttal sprang to mind, but that wasn't the word that emerged. She removed the last costume. "Yes."

Ryan rolled off the bed and extended his hand. When she took it, his fingers threaded through hers, filling her with warmth. He led her to the bathroom and turned on the shower without releasing her hand. Tugging her to him, he pressed a soft kiss on her lips. "Thank you for giving me this second chance. I won't let you down."

Julia nodded. She wanted him so much, needed him to drive away the loneliness and the chill that had encased her for months now.

A sense of wonder filled Ryan when she settled against him, naked, chest to chest, with warm water pouring down over their heads. It was home and every part of him rejoiced at having his wife in his arms again. He kissed her cheek and sucked at the juncture of her neck and shoulder. Touching her was like sticking his finger in a light bulb socket, or at least how he imagined that experience.

His wife.

The woman who'd spoiled him for all others.

He skimmed his hand down her back and cupped her bottom, drawing her against his straining erection. From zero to go in half a second. Her tongue darted out to lick along the tail of his dragon tatt, over one pectoral muscle before settling against his nipple. Pleasure snared him, dragging another groan to the surface. Urgency thrummed through his body now, and Julia seemed just as caught in the writhing emotions as he. He lifted her and her legs curled around his waist. Still the water poured over them. He sucked roughly on one breast, and she jerked, almost ripping out a handful of hair when he tried to reposition his mouth to her other breast.

"Ryan," she whispered hoarsely, full of silent pleading.

Hell, he didn't want to wait either.

Angling his body, he pressed her against the wall.

"Cold," she muttered.

"Won't be soon." He gripped his cock, positioned himself at her entrance and let gravity impale her more deeply. Ryan gritted his teeth, the snug warmth of her almost doing him in. His balls pulled tight. His pulse raced, his heart threatening to beat right out of his chest as Julia's pussy flexed around his shaft and took him inside her. "Okay?" he demanded.

"No! Wait," she said. "Condom."

"Shit." He stilled, grunting as he squeezed her against the wall. It took everything in him, but he withdrew and set her on her feet, maintaining his grip on her shoulders. "Sorry. I didn't think." He'd presumed she was still on the Pill. She had taken them when they first married. He leaned down, then pressed his forehead against hers while catching his breath. A child was strangely appealing, but he didn't voice his thoughts, not when Julia hadn't seemed happy at the idea. "Turn around. Let me wash your back."

She bit her lip and turned to present her back. He grabbed a bottle of body wash and squirted some on a bath buddy. Seconds later, his hand was covered with lather.

"I said I was sorry. There's no need to give me the silent treatment."

"I'm not." She turned in his arms, a strange expression on her face. "I'm just as much to blame." She took the buddy off him and indicated he should turn around.

Ryan turned, sighing, sorry the mood had passed. "Are you still going to let me make love to you?" He winced at his bluntness.

"I have condoms in the bedroom."

His breath caught. "Why?"

"I bought them a few months ago when I decided I should have sex with someone to forget you."

"Ouch." Her words hurt, but given his lack of communication, he didn't blame her. "And did you find a man?" She'd implied she hadn't had sex for months, but perhaps he'd misunderstood.

"No. You done?" The defensive note told him not to push.

He washed the last of the soap away. "Yeah, I'm done."

After toweling off, he padded to her bedroom. While he was waiting for her, he pulled back the covers, desire simmering inside him at the idea of touching her again, despite his confused feelings. From the deep recesses of his mind he pulled an image of her naked, stroking scented body butter on her legs, one at a time. He recalled the slow caress of her hands, smoothing across her skin. It was so real—a true memory. He grinned, absently fondling his cock.

"Having sex with you doesn't mean I'm agreeing to continue our marriage," she said abruptly as she entered the bedroom.

"What does it mean?" Ryan didn't understand the brittle edge to her voice, the pain she was trying to hide.

"I'm scratching an itch."

Okay. Ryan forced a smile even though a part of him died. He'd done this. Even though he hadn't meant to—his silence had hurt her and damaged their relationship. "Fair enough. Let's do that scratching together." Her bitchiness was a façade. He was sure of it.

"All right." She dropped her towel and crossed the room to the bedside cabinet. She opened the drawer and pulled out a box of condoms. An unopened box, he noted, and some of the tightness in his chest dispersed.

"Come here," he said in a rough voice. He sat on the edge of the bed and waited for her to approach, another level of tension easing when she came willingly enough. She wanted him. At least they had the sexual part of their marriage to help glue their relationship together. He could fix this if he loved her hard enough.

His avid gaze took in everything about her. God, she was

beautiful with her trim waist and long legs. He drew her between his legs, pressing a kiss to the slight round of her belly, just below her belly button piercing. She froze, but he ignored her reaction to draw her down onto his lap. He settled his mouth on hers despite the hint of frost in her. Determined to break her reserve, he doubled his effort, sliding his tongue against hers, tangling his fingers in her hair and tasting the mint from recently brushed teeth.

A few seconds later, she moaned against his mouth—music to his ears. Her hands slid over his shoulders and suddenly she was taking part instead of letting him touch her. Her breasts squashed against the wall of his chest, the eager pressure of her lips drawing a heated response from him. Yes, perfect, and he settled in to enjoy playing tag with her tongue.

They kissed, unhurried now that they were naked and near a bed and condoms. Long, lazy kisses. Slow, seductive kisses until they were both breathing hard, and his cock was so rigid he knew he'd explode if he didn't get inside her soon.

He shifted, tossing her on the mattress and covering her before she had time to protest.

"I need you, Julia." He ran a finger up the soft skin of her inner thigh. He'd wait a little longer. Make this extra special for both of them. He shifted back, setting between the V of her legs to study her pussy and the narrow strip of blonde hair. So pretty. Where to start? Licking, he decided, and immediately ran his tongue from her entrance and up to her clit. Not a soft fluttery lick, but a hard, firm one that filled his mouth with her taste and stopped short of her clitoris. He lifted his head to grin up at her. "How's that?"

"Good," she whispered, arching her hips upward to increase the pressure. "Ryan!"

Still grinning, Ryan settled in to make her come. Not that it was an arduous task. She was swollen and trembled whenever his tongue neared her clit. He teased her for a while with slow, delicate laps, keeping her on edge but not giving her enough stimulation to topple into climax. Her juices seeped from her entrance, her spicy taste filling his mouth while pleading cries spilled from her lips.

"Oh, Ryan." Her hands gripped his head to focus his touch.

He glanced up to find her eyes squeezed closed, her bottom lip caught between her white teeth as her lower body strained upward, pushing into his face.

"Please. Please, Ryan."

Aware of urgency thrumming through his own veins, he continued, this time concentrating on the straining bundle of nerves. Carefully, he took the bud between his lips, stroking with a barely-there touch of his tongue. She shuddered, groaned and fought to raise her hips, forcing him into greater contact. He gave it to her. Laving back and forth. Sucking carefully.

She cried out, trembled and the tiny bud vibrated in

rapid spasms. He kept his touches light now, vaguely remembering this was what she enjoyed.

The tension melted from her limbs and torso, and she sagged in a sprawl on the mattress. "Oh, Ryan. That was an A-grade orgasm." Her throaty whisper brought a burst of satisfaction, like a jolt to the chest, and he smiled before pressing a light kiss to her sensitive clit.

Ryan fumbled with the outer wrapping of the condom box before he extracted a foil packet. Seconds later the latex was in place. He moved up her body, touched his lips to hers and slipped inside her. It was like coming home. Ryan moved and her hips shifted in counterpoint. The tight clench around his shaft forced a moan from deep in his chest. His breath caught as he watched her face, the minute shifts of expression as she started the climb to a peak again. He stroked into her faster, hurling himself greedily into the pleasure of the experience. She filled the gaps inside him, the loneliness. God, she made him whole.

Her arms wrapped around him, holding him tight. Ryan grunted, slammed into her. Once. Twice. And a third time, then his orgasm roared through him, white noise echoing in his ears. His lips sought hers again, anchoring himself in the present.

Aw, sweet. So sweet. He withdrew a fraction and pushed back into her heat. Lazy, easy thrusts even though he'd come. Julia groaned, her hips lifting. Taking her subtle clue, he reached between them and stroked her clitoris.

"Yes. Right there. No! Don't move." She grabbed his ears and tugged.

"Ow, woman. Bossy much?"

"Get me off," she ordered.

Laughter spilled from him along with contentment. His finger worked her, and he watched her face again. Her eyes fluttered closed, arousal colored her cheeks in a delicate pink. Her lips were swollen. Her blonde hair tousled. Sexy. She came, shuddering and squeezing his cock in rhythmic pulses, looking beautiful.

"Was that up to your expectations?" he whispered after he'd withdrawn and dealt with the condom. He tucked her against the curve of his body.

Julia yawned. "Hmm, I need to get some sleep."

Some of his feel-good attitude dispersed. He opened his mouth to say something, to ask if she hadn't enjoyed their lovemaking before reconsidering. Crap, questions would make him sound needy and lacking in self-confidence. Him. The guy who, according to Caleb, charmed females of every age with nothing more than a smile. The guy who fronted *French Letters* and held their fans in thrall. The man voted sexiest scoundrel for the last two years in a row by *Madam* magazine.

Julia's deep, even breathing indicated she'd fallen asleep while he felt like a theatre prop—an object present to illustrate a point.

The next morning, Ryan woke alone. Gritty eyed, he sat

up. "Julia?"

Frowning, he scrambled out of bed and padded to the bathroom. The faint scent of Julia's perfume filled the air, but by the time he reached the kitchen he realized he was alone in the apartment.

"Damn." He stomped back to the spare bedroom, indignation in every rapid step. He might have slept with a lot of women before Julia came along, but he was pretty sure he'd never sneaked out before they woke or left them feeling cheap and used.

CHAPTER EIGHT

"THEY CAN'T DO THIS." Julia strode across her mother's bedroom, shaking the letter from the bank in her hand. She'd popped in early to see her mother and hadn't expected a bombshell to greet her. She turned back to face her mother and Janet. "I've paid off the arrears. All the payments are up to date."

Janet sent her a warning glance, one that told her she needed to pull herself together for her mother's sake. Janet was right of course. Her mother needed tranquility now that her operation was scheduled.

"They can call in the loan. It's in the small print." Regret weighted her mother's demeanor. "I didn't want things to end this way."

"I'll talk with them," Julia said. "I'll take Susan. She's good with financial stuff. We'll show them the budgets Susan has done and tell them about the bookings we've lined up already."

The lines on her mother's pale face deepened and her posture sagged inward. "I'm sorry, Julia. This mess is my fault."

Janet sat on the bed and took Elise's hand. "Don't worry. Julia will take care of everything."

Julia sought her mother's gaze and held it, pushing out confidence despite the quivers of fear dive-bombing like fishing seabirds in the pit of her stomach. "It's not your fault, Mum. We're on target to open this weekend instead of next. We intend to use the first week as a trial to sort out teething problems and have our grand opening night as I'd originally planned. I'll ring the bank and arrange an appointment." She folded the bank letter and tucked it into the pocket of her jacket. "How are you doing this morning?"

"Janet and I are going out for breakfast. I fancy some fresh air," her mother said, still looking as if she blamed herself.

"That's wonderful," Julia said in a bracing voice. She would fix this if it killed her because she hated seeing the defeat sitting on her parent's strong shoulders, weighing her down when she needed to focus on her health. "Do you need help getting dressed?" She didn't ask if her mother was strong enough for the outing, despite thinking it. Her mother deserved sunshine in her life after working hard for as long as Julia could remember.

"Janet and I will manage." Her voice regained a fraction of her normal determination.

Julia brushed a kiss over her mum's cheek. "I'll leave you to it then. I'll be in the club if you need me for anything."

She spent the next two hours practicing a dance routine and going through arrangements for their first private function.

Susan, Christina and Maggie arrived together and joined her practice. The music came to an end and they stopped, panting with exertion.

"That was brilliant," Susan said. "I managed the entire routine without a mistake."

"Did you get your confirmation from *Farmer Seeks a Wife*?" Christina asked.

"You've received more details?" Maggie demanded.

Susan nodded, looking a little sick. "The first elimination event is in two months."

"Where is the event? What do you have to do? Spill already." Maggie glowered a little. "Don't make me pull the deets out of you."

Christina took a deep breath. "They're busing us to a vineyard at Matakana, north of Auckland. Each of the farmers speed dates his group of girls, and he'll pick his eight favorites."

"What should I wear?" Susan wailed. "I'm so nervous I'll fluff my speed date. Remember the speed dating thing we attended last year? I sucked."

"We'll practice mini interviews with you," Julia said. "The clothes thing is easy because we have an expert in our midst. You should see the costumes Christina has picked out for our routine. They're—"

Ryan and Caleb walked into the club, both carrying guitar cases.

"They're what?" Maggie asked.

Julia ripped her gaze off Ryan and turned back to her friends. "Glamorous. They're gorgeous and yet sexy too."

"Morning," Caleb said in a loud voice.

Ryan waved, and they continued to the stage. The guitars came out, and soon music filled the club.

"They're fantastic," Christina said, wiggling her hips and swaying to the beat. Her bracelets jingled. "I'd buy their music."

She already had. Julia sighed, unaccountably disappointed because Ryan hadn't come over and said good morning. "Susan, the bank has called in the loan. I need to make an appointment and go armed with budgets and lots of information to argue my case."

Susan gasped. "I thought you brought the loan up to date."

"I did." And she'd used all her cash reserves to do it.

"ATTENTION ON THE MUSIC," Caleb said.

Ryan scowled as Julia strode out of the club with her friend Susan. "I didn't realize...I thought I'd be able to talk her around without breaking a sweat." *Bigheaded oaf.*

"Your usual charm offensive not working for you?"

"Not as well as I'd hoped. I'm not sure what to do next."

"Have you tried sex?"

"Yes." His tone emerged curt with a whiff of pissed.

"Interesting. You could give up," Caleb said, strumming several chords and making a notation on the music sheet.

"No." Ryan stood and shoved his guitar back in its case. "This song isn't working right. I need a break. Have you met Julia's mother?"

"No."

"Come and meet her now."

They met Elise and her friend Janet at the base of the stairs.

"We're going out for a late breakfast," Elise said. "Why don't you come with us?"

"Caleb?" Ryan turned to his mate. "How would you like to escort these two lovely ladies on their outing?"

"Sounds good," Caleb said.

The Viaduct was quieter than usual since it was a weekday and not yet mid-morning. The late summer sun sent sparkles of light dancing over the water, and the foursome settled at an outside table to watch the activity on the two luxury yachts moored nearby.

"I love a water view," Elise said.

"Once you've recovered from the operation, we'll go to Fiji," Janet said. "Imagine the white sand and the glorious sunsets."

Elise frowned. "I'm not sure I can afford to go now."

"Why not?" Ryan asked.

"The bank has called in the loan. There was plenty of money to cover it, but my last manager did a runner after cleaning me out. The police haven't found him," Elise said. "Julia has made an appointment to see the bank manager today."

Caleb and Ryan exchanged a quick look. They had stacks of money.

"Julia didn't tell me," Ryan said. "She was gone when I woke up this morning."

Janet made a *tsking* sound at the back of her throat. "She's working too hard."

"I know this is nosy," Ryan said, "but how much is the loan? What is Julia going to do if the bank won't relent?"

Elise frowned. "She told me not to worry and said she'd work out something."

"The loan is just under fifty thousand," Janet said. "Elise and I can't put any more money into the business. We might have to sell."

"I can give you the money," Ryan said.

"But why would you want to—" Elise broke off when the waitress arrived with their coffee.

"Julia is my wife," Ryan said.

"I can help out with money too," Caleb said. "No," he added when it looked as if the women would turn down their offer. "Call it a loan. Both Ryan and I have seen what Julia's done so far. Her ideas and the changes she's made are good. She already has bookings. From my side of the fence the club seems an excellent investment."

"Give me your bank account number," Ryan said. "I'll transfer the money today."

Elise shot a quick glance at Janet before tipping a sachet of sugar into her coffee and giving it a vigorous stir. She tapped her spoon on the side of the cup and lifted her head. "Julia might argue. I know my daughter, and I can see you have problems with your marriage. I don't want to land in the middle of a disagreement."

"It's true we've had issues. I won't deny it." Ryan said. "We're working through them. Elise, I love your daughter, and I have no intention of walking away from her again."

Janet and Elise exchanged another long look, doing heavy duty communication he didn't understand. Ryan's mouth dried while he waited for their decision. He'd do whatever he had to do, whether they approved or not.

"All right," Janet said. "I suppose I could tell Julia the money came from me."

"We'll play it by ear," Elise suggested and beamed at both men. "Thank you."

"I'm sorry, Ms. Maxwell." The loan officer used a forefinger to push his spotlessly clean glasses up his nose.

"I understand your account is now up to date, but your club has been losing money steadily during the past three years. You are closed at present, which doesn't foster my confidence."

"We have current budgets and cash forecasts for the next two years," Susan said. "We intend to turn the club around."

"A salient point, but I'm afraid it changes nothing. The bank requires you to repay the loan in full by the date stated in our letter. If you do not meet your obligations, we will take up our security and liquidate all assets."

Julia scanned the man's ruddy, determined face and realized nothing they said would make any difference. He'd decided and wasn't about to change to their point of view. She stood and inclined her head in a polite manner while she fantasized about punching him in the nose. "Thank you for seeing us."

Susan followed her out of the bank and grasped her elbow once they were outside. "Can we try to refinance?"

"That's the only alternative we have."

"I'll do some research for you," Susan said. "Tell you your options then we can make appointments for tomorrow."

"Thanks, Susan."

Susan gave a dismissive shrug. "I believe in the club. You will make it work. You deserve this chance, and I want to help you every way I can. We all want to help and see you succeed."

Julia gave Susan a quick hug, the tingling warmth of her friend's words helping cushion her disappointment as they headed back to the club. Music poured through the door when they entered. Ryan and Caleb were practicing again. Christina had stenciled the walls with gold paint and was instructing several helpers.

"The gold borders look fantastic," Susan said.

"They do." Julia did a slow turn and nodded approval. It was amazing what a difference a paintjob made to the cavernous room. "I'd better see Mum, tell her the bad news."

Susan squeezed her arm and flashed a smile full of confidence. "Try not to worry. I'll find a way to refinance, and we'll be back in business in no time."

Julia climbed the stairs to the flat, and on the threshold, she took a bracing breath and plastered a smile on her face. "How was the breakfast?"

"It was lovely getting out in the fresh air. Ryan and Caleb went with us. We were the envy of every woman in the vicinity," her mother said, a sparkle in her eyes and a healthy blush of pleasure on her cheeks for a change. "I like your young man."

"I like him too," Julia said absently while she tried to work the angles. Why would Ryan and Caleb take two elderly women out for a jaunt?

"I should hope so," her mother said tartly. "You married

him. In secret, I might add. You still haven't explained the why of your hurried wedding."

Julia's heart twisted, then the traitorous organ seemed to plunge as if she were falling down a cliff. She sucked in a hasty breath, knowing she owed her mother explanations. "I...I was scared," she said. "And Ryan, he sort of snuck up on me. I wanted to spend every moment with him, and marriage seemed a good idea."

"But you didn't stay together."

"No. There are things I can't tell you. I promised."

Elise nodded. "Why were you frightened?"

Yikes, straight for the throat. "Growing up, the kids at school teased me about the club. It embarrassed me. Every man I met who knew about the club treated me like a tramp. You know, the usual stuff. I thought Ryan might react the same way so I didn't tell him."

"But he knows now." Janet exchanged a glance with Elise.

"Yes." Julia frowned as she took in their expressions. "What are you keeping from me?"

Her mother ignored the question. "Did you tell him about Lucas and what the slimy bastard did to you?"

"No."

"Secrets aren't good in a relationship," her mother said and shot a quick glance at Janet. "The pair of you should talk."

Ryan. Something in her mother's expression told her

he'd done something she wouldn't approve of. Without saying another word, she wheeled around and stomped down the stairs to the club. God, every single one of her problems started with the pesky man. The scent of paint wafted to meet her when she turned the corner and stormed toward the stage. Caleb noticed her first and stopped playing.

"Why did you stop—" Ryan glanced up and caught sight of her. His lips curled into his usual smile—the one that oozed charm and charisma and made a woman's panties dampen as she considered what it would take to tame him.

Julia scowled, ignoring the sucker punch to her equilibrium. Her hands curled to fists to halt the impulse to knock his grin off his face. "What?" she demanded in a low growl.

Ryan's smile lost some of its *oomph*. "I have no idea what you're talking about."

"While you were out with my mother and Janet, you did something. What did you do?"

"Caleb and I have paid off your loan." He didn't bother to sugarcoat the truth of his interference.

"Why?" It was a howl of frustration, of anger, and her cry held pain too. She'd wanted to fix everything herself, even if the problems seemed insurmountable.

"Julia, Ryan and I have the money, and we wanted to help. It's as simple as that," Caleb said in a reasonable tone.

"You can either pay us back when you're able to or we can be silent partners."

"You didn't think to ask first?" Julia didn't take her gaze off Ryan.

"Your mother was worried," he said. "She doesn't need that sort of stress when she has her heart problem to deal with."

The punch seeped out of her argument. He was right. "Fine," she gritted out. "I'll pay you back every cent."

CHAPTER NINE

JULIA SULKED ABOUT HIS interference for the next three days, only speaking to him when necessary. They lived in the same house and traveled to the club together, yet she continued to give him the silent treatment.

He'd had enough.

Ryan waited until she finished her shower and returned to her bedroom. He took a quick shower, pulled on a pair of boxer-briefs and headed for her room ready to have the subject out with her. If that meant an argument then too bad. He was sick of damn pussyfooting around her.

He rapped on the door, waited an instant. Of course she didn't invite him in. Bugger that. He shoved the door open and stormed inside. "I want our marriage to work. I was trying to help, damn it."

"I know." Julia reclined on the bed and looked as miserable as he'd felt since their confrontation.

"I don't want to argue with you."

She sat up, then climbed under the covers and propped a pillow behind her for greater comfort. "I wish you and Caleb had talked to me first."

"Would you have accepted our money?"

Her forehead scrunched up as she hesitated. "I don't know. Maybe. But you didn't give me a chance because you took the decision out of my hands."

"Look, we're both new to this marriage business. We're going to make mistakes."

"Not me," she said, but her cheeks reddened at the patent untruth.

"No? You don't think you jumped to conclusions without giving me the benefit of the doubt?"

"We're not talking about the loan anymore," she said in a flat voice.

"No."

"I tried to ring you. I tried to email you. I even called your manager. Then there were the photos." She sucked in a deep breath, staring down at her hands. "When I was twenty-one I got engaged. The entire time my fiancé was cheating on me. His actions might have colored my reaction to you."

News to him. "How did you discover he was cheating?"

"An STD. I hadn't slept with anyone else, which meant he had."

"Hell," Ryan said.

"Yeah."

Indignation filled him on her behalf and a slice of pissed too, at her dumping a crappy past at his door and judging him by the same standards as her ex. He hadn't damn well cheated on her, hadn't looked at another woman. "I didn't deserve that."

"No, you didn't," she said, eyes narrowing when he sent her a stink eye. "Don't you think I know that? How unfair I'm being? I can't help it. The guilt—" Her lips pressed together, and she gave an irritable shrug. "It's cold tonight. Why don't you get into bed with me?"

Her casual suggestion took some of the ginger out of his mood, but not enough to make his mind stop working. "Why are you guilty?"

When she ignored his question, Ryan slid under the covers and slithered closer. Perhaps pushing his luck, he wrapped his arms around her and drew her against his chest. To his relief she gave a tired sigh and relaxed into his embrace. "We should make a pact," he whispered against her hair.

"And that would be?"

"We need to talk about things instead of jumping to conclusions. We will never build trust between us if we don't share our thoughts."

"I know. I'm guilty of running away and hiding my head in the sand." Her voice was muffled against his shoulder. "I told you I tried to contact you while the band was in

Europe."

"But you understand the lack of communication was a mistake, a one off. It will never happen again."

"I do. A comedy of errors."

Ryan snorted. "Black errors." His fingers roved her back. "I've hated sleeping alone during the last couple of nights."

"I needed time to—"

"Sulk?"

"Maybe." She huffed out a laugh. "Should I make it up to you?"

"Depends." He nuzzled her neck and took two tiny bites of her silky skin. "Are we good now? Do you forgive me? Are you going to throw our money back in our faces?"

"That would be silly of me. Now that the debt is cleared, I'll go into the reopening with a clean slate. I won't have the pressure of keeping up the loan payments."

"Caleb and I want to test out a couple of our songs with an audience. Would you let us provide some of the music?"

"I'd be stupid to turn you away, but aren't you worried about blowing your cover? You go to so much trouble hiding your identities."

"We've made excellent progress on our new arrangements. Neil and Jeff will return to Auckland any day now, and we need to practice. Caleb and I figured if we do covers combined with a few of our new songs, that would work. Would you let us try?"

"I'd be silly to say no." She licked across his collarbone

and wriggled against him.

"So we have a deal about discussing things that irk us instead of reacting with our guts or sulking?"

"We have a deal," she said and lifted her head to seal it with a kiss. It was slow and steamy and streaked electricity to his cock. She took the kiss deeper, twining her tongue with his until he could think of nothing but pushing into her tight warmth.

When she lifted her head, he gripped her shoulders to draw her close again.

"No," she whispered. "Let me." Julia scooted under the covers and licked one nipple. Her hair grazed his skin as she moved lower. Her hands were everywhere, moving across his thighs, his belly and pinching his butt.

He let out a yelp, which turned into a strangled moan when the heat of her mouth surrounded the tip of his erection. When her tongue came into play, sensible flew from his mind and he focused on the sensations. She stroked him with an expertise that tossed him into turmoil, had his balls tightening and a steady stream of pre-come leaking from his slit. She teased him until he shuddered, his cock so full and tight he wondered if he might burst out of his skin. His hand slipped down to cradle her head, his fingers sliding into her silky hair.

"Take me inside you," he whispered. "Ride me."

She released his shaft with a distinct pop, and thankfully wriggled up his body. She reached into the bedside drawer for a condom and rolled it down his shaft with quick proficiency. Ryan swallowed, savoring her innate beauty with her messy blonde hair, her sparkling brown eyes and swollen mouth, aware of how lucky he was to have her in his arms.

He stared at her as she guided him to her and sank down an increment at a time. She flexed around him, clutching his shaft when she rose and fell. She increased her pace, sliding her fingers down her body to get herself off.

A moan slipped from her lips, and she threw her head back, freezing with his cock partially embedded in her pussy. Her inner muscles squeezed his shaft, and she gasped.

Her brown eyes opened, and she winked at him. "Nice moves."

"Do I get a reward for holding back?"

The corners of her eyes crinkled. "You didn't have to." She lifted her weight and slid back down again with more force. "How is that?"

"Like you're strangling my cock."

She chuckled and he gripped her hips, yanking her down on his dick, so close to release stars flashed behind his closed eyes. He lifted her and pulled her down again and came, his climax taking him to the knife edge of pain, yet the pleasure swelled through him until he felt as if he were exploding through the air. He came down gradually and sent Julia a lazy smile of satisfaction.

"That was amazing."

"It was good on my side too." She slipped off him and padded to the bathroom. While he removed the condom, he heard the water turn on and off again. She returned minutes later with a glass of water, her throat working as she swallowed it down.

"Do you want a glass?"

"Sure."

She disappeared and returned, handing the water to him. "I'm getting excited about opening night. Did you still want to play at the hen's night?"

"Yes. It would just be Caleb and me."

Julia nodded and crawled under the covers. She cuddled against him with a sigh.

Ryan pressed a kiss to her temple. "Good night, sweetheart."

Julia closed her eyes. "Good night."

She sensed the moment Ryan fell asleep. Her muscles ached from exercise and exhaustion pulled at her mind. Yet she was nowhere near falling asleep. She'd had the perfect opportunity to tell him about their baby, but even after their discussion about honesty and openness, she'd choked. Heck, she'd opened her mouth to confess, but the lump in her throat had prevented her from speaking. And the longer she'd left it, the harder it was to tell him about the child she'd wanted so badly, about the never-ending guilt inside her. A tear squeezed free and ran down her cheek.

Maybe she'd tell him another time.

Anguish twisted in her as she recalled the baby she'd lost. Another tear escaped, and she let it, crying for the past and lost opportunities.

THE HEN'S NIGHT PASSED without a hitch, and the women loved the burlesque lessons. They were equally complimentary about the music and the routines Julia and the other dancers did for them. Now it was the unofficial opening night. As Julia had planned, they'd saved the advertising for the following weekend, wanting to iron out any problems before they attempted to attract customers.

"Are you sure you want to dance tonight?" Julia asked Christina and Susan.

"Heck yeah," Susan said. "It was such a rush dancing at the hen's night."

"You just want the gazes of the male customers crawling over you," Maggie said.

"Ah, but they won't recognize me," Susan said triumphantly. "Not when I'm wearing a wig, a sexy mask and one of the classy costumes Christina has organized."

"But their eyes will still crawl over you," Maggie pointed out. "And not in a good way."

Susan grinned. "You're just ticked because Connor won't let you dance. You've spouted his reasons."

Maggie rubbed her backside, her manner rueful. "I'm allowed to help out if Julia is desperate, but I have to seek his permission first. He was clear about that."

Susan poked her fingers in her ears. "La. La. La."

"Have you found more dancers?" Christina asked.

Julia sighed. "No, and it's a worry. I can't be here all the time, and I can't keep relying on my friends to fill in the gaps." She glanced at Susan. "Even if they're naturals on the stage."

"There!" Susan said, snapping her fingers at Maggie. "Julia said I'm a natural." Her eyes glowed with pleasure.

"Nothing less than the truth," Julia said. "Anyone have any ideas about where to find more dancers?"

"Have you tried some of the dancing schools?" Christina asked. "Now that there's no stripping involved, some of the dancers might take an interest in earning money doing burlesque."

Julia clapped a hand to her head. "Why didn't I think of that? I still take a few classes between my keep-fit sessions. I'll ask the school owner." She hurried off, aware of the low hum of nerves in the pit of her stomach. She'd either thrive or sink in obscurity after the formal opening night because she had no intention of borrowing more money from Ryan. It was a point of pride.

A ten-minute chat later, she was back with a bounce

in her step. "The owner asked for volunteers and I have ten dancers arriving in an hour." She clapped her hands together. "Maggie, will you cue the music?"

The day passed way too quickly with the thousand and one details she needed to take care of before they opened to the public.

Now, at eight in the evening, Julia took a deep breath and opened the front door to *Maxwell's*.

Stan, her doorman, switched on the new neon sign and walked outside to view the bright violet against black. "That's real classy, Miss Julia."

She nodded, pleased with the effect. "It looks stylish."

"I hope it's enough to attract the crowds. It would be nice to have a queue like the opposition," he said.

Julia's eyes narrowed on the premises of their closest competitor. "I wonder if we should rent a crowd for the official opening night."

"Elise used to distribute flyers with a coupon for a free drink."

"That might work," Julia mused, glancing down at her black trouser suit. Professional? Yes, but she needed in-your-face sexy for this situation. "But for the next few nights I'm going to try the old-fashioned carnival way. I'll be back in a sec." She strode back into the club, spying Connor and Maggie standing by the stage.

"Connor, just the person I wanted to see. I need your help. Maggie, can I borrow him? He might need to flirt with a few women, but I promise there will be no touching involved."

Maggie shot her husband a considering glance. A crafty expression darted over her face before a toothy grin bloomed. "Will you let me dance? I enjoy it, and I promise to keep my clothes on."

"On the condition you do some of the raunchy stuff for me," Connor said.

Maggie let out a screech of excitement. "Deal."

"I feel as if I should put my fingers in my ears like Susan does," Julia said drily. "You can say no if you want."

"Watching Maggie dance makes me proud," Connor said. "It's the other men who make me see red. I don't like the idea of others fantasizing about touching my wife." He studied Maggie, and the faint tension in the air dispersed. "But, the truth is she's good and enjoys the challenge. All of you are great. What do you want me to do?"

Julia chuckled. "Don't you mean you're seeing green?"

"I've seen you scowl when women look at your husband," he shot back.

"Yes, well, moving on. I need Christina to deck you out in a sexy costume." She stood back to consider him, her head cocked to the side. "Vampire, I think. I'll dress the glamorous lady vamp, and we'll go out the front and talk up the place to passersby. Flirt and tease a little and tell them about our sexy dancers."

"Let me do it," Ryan said from behind her. "Please."

Julia swiveled to face him and nodded slowly, melting under his intent gaze. "All right."

"Do you want Caleb to come and provide music?"

"Yes please," Julia said. "That would be a nice touch."

"Let's go," Ryan said, holding out his hand. Her heart skipped a beat when his fingers wrapped around hers, and together, she and Ryan followed Christina out the back to the dressing room. He still had the knack of turning her breathless whenever he switched on his charm, and she wondered if she should worry, because the charisma translated to females of all ages. Scowling, she forced away the faint apprehension to focus on the present. He hadn't put a foot wrong, and he deserved her trust.

Christina went straight to the racks of costumes. "Slinky red for you." She handed the silky dress to Julia. "And a red shirt to go with Ryan's black trousers."

Julia stripped off her clothes and wriggled into the form-fitting dress while Ryan traded his shirt with the one Christina gave him. When they were both dressed, Christina stood back and nodded.

"Perfect." Christina made shooing motions with her hands. "Go. Bring us some customers."

By the time they exited the dressing room, half a dozen customers had walked into the club. Music blared through the speakers and one of her original dancers appeared on stage. Julia was pleased to see the effort she'd put into training had improved the dancer's routine and her attitude. When the dancer caught her eye, Julia gave her a thumbs up gesture.

"Julia." Ryan's soft voice drew her attention.

"Yes?" The instant she met his gaze her knees threatened to buckle. Although they continued to sleep together, she held part of herself back. Ryan would leave soon to go on tour, and she wasn't sure she'd hold herself together, if she could allow herself to trust him. Yeah. It was stupid, letting her fears ride her, but she couldn't seem to put her misgivings behind her. She swallowed, promising herself she'd try harder.

"Don't be nervous. You've put so much work into the club." He squeezed her shoulder, a gesture of additional support. "You won't fail."

"Am I that obvious?"

"No, you come across confident in your decisions. You forget I know you well."

"We have spent so little time together."

"Is that what's bothering you?"

Julia glanced at him, indecision tossing her around in a maelstrom of worries and apprehension. "No matter how you talk around the situation, we still have the same problems."

"This time you'll have the support of your friends, and I'll have Caleb. Not that you have to worry," he added. "What I mean is we'll both have a better safety network."

She drew in a quick breath. "Keep reassuring me so the

past doesn't come back to whack me over the head, okay?"

"Deal."

"Okay, you have my permission to unleash your charm and flirt with the girls. I'll do the same with the men. We'll get Caleb to play and start with a dance or two."

Caleb was waiting for them when they reached the front door. Outside, the night was starting to creep in, and the neon lights along K' Road sparkled like an elderly lady in fancy dress. It was too early for the streetwalkers, but in a few more hours, they'd pop out of the woodwork.

"Music to tango to," Julia said, already knowing Ryan could dance. They'd tangoed in Fiji under the moonlight. It was one of her favorite memories, and the hot sex in their bungalow afterward hadn't hurt either.

Caleb grinned in their direction, his nimble fingers plucking out the sultry notes of a Latin number. Ryan drew her nearer and led her into the steps. Across the street a group of young women stopped to watch. Ryan, ever the charmer, flashed a smile in their direction and dipped Julia. The women hooted approval and crossed the street when the light halted traffic.

Julia and Ryan kept dancing, flowing into some showy moves. The crowd increased, and by the time Caleb came to the end of the song with a flourish, they stood in a circle three deep.

Julia sucked in air, her breathing rapid despite her fitness. Ryan curved his arm around her shoulders, his scent and heat surrounding her.

"Are you going clubbing tonight?" Ryan directed his question to the young women who'd stopped to watch them first.

"Girls' night out," a cute redhead said. Her eyelashes fluttered as she peeked up at him in a flirtatious manner.

"Why don't you start your night here?" Ryan asked.

One of the redhead's friends wrinkled her nose. "This place is a dive."

Julia opened her mouth to refute the point, but Ryan squeezed her in warning.

"The place has received a revamp, and I personally vouch for the new manager. They have a new lineup of dancers and routines. You should try them."

The redhead made a scoffing sound. "You have to say that. You work there."

"I'm helping out for a few weeks," Ryan said. "I'm not on the payroll."

"Do you have a girlfriend?" the redhead asked with another flutter of her stick-on lashes.

"He has a wife," Julia said sweetly. Damn. She bit down on her lip. *Way to attract new customers.*

"I don't have a girlfriend," Caleb said.

"Is it worth trying out this club?" the redhead asked.

"Yes," Caleb said.

Two couples from the group wandered off, and Julia wanted to run after them and drag them back. They stopped by *Maxwell's* closest opposition, took in the length of the line and had a quick discussion before retracing their steps.

"Score one for the new club," Julia murmured.

Most of the people who'd stopped to watch them dance ended up walking inside, ready to try the new place.

"Fantastic job, guys," Julia said to Ryan and Caleb.

"Should we sing?" Ryan whispered into her ear.

"A ballad," she suggested. "Something I can do a simple routine to."

"Yes, ma'am," Caleb said, strumming his guitar.

Ryan and Caleb's voices blended into a thing of beauty. Closing her eyes, Julia attempted to shrug off her earlier jealousy when the redhead had flirted with Ryan. When the emotion lingered, she gave it a harder shove, scooting it to the back of her mind. After another breath, she started to move to the beat of the music, lifting her hands and clicking her fingers while two of the members of *French Letters* sang of love and candy sweet kisses.

Julia had to force herself to open her eyes and watch for potential customers. As she'd hoped, their singing, dancing and patter attracted attention, and many of those who spied the line outside their opposition decided to give *Maxwell's* a try instead of queuing.

By the time she'd hustled and danced outside for an hour, they'd enticed a respectable number of customers inside.

"That should do it for now," she said, pleased with this way of attracting patrons. "That worked well. I need to consider hiring hosts and hostesses to entice people into the club."

"You might need to hire additional security," Ryan said.

"I'd prefer not to, but Stan would need help if we had troublesome customers."

Ryan brushed his fingers over her cheek and resettled a flyaway lock of air. "I'd feel better if you had muscle on the premises to thwart any idiocy."

He meant when he left to do the concert in Wellington, and the others their manager had booked for them in Australia. "I'll contemplate security and discuss it with Mum. She might have some ideas."

Lucky for her, Ryan took her diversion and ran with it. "Did she enjoy the dress rehearsal for the dancers? You didn't say."

Julia nodded, the quick sting of tears coming to her eyes. "She told me she was proud of what I'd achieved."

"She likes having you around."

"She makes me guilty for leaving her to run the place alone all these years."

Ryan brushed his knuckles over her cheeks. "No. If she realized you thought that way she'd be upset. You needed to stretch your wings and do something else. Elise gave you the opportunity to follow your dreams."

"Huh! Big dreams. I attended secretarial college."

Ryan grinned. "Caleb and I didn't stay at university for long. Pissed the parents right off. They're a bit happier now, although they harp on about saving money for a rainy day."

When they entered the club Susan was on stage going through one of her routines. Julia nodded approvingly at the way her friend threw herself into the role and became a sultry seductress with one click of her fingers and the cock of a hip. Behind her mask, her eyes smoldered with heat.

"She's a natural," Ryan said. "The guys can't keep their eyes off her."

"The women either. They want to be her," Julia said with distinct satisfaction. And it was good for Susan too. She radiated confidence and her propensity for judging people harshly hadn't appeared for ages. Her friend had bloomed.

"I'd better join Caleb." He kissed her lightly on the lips and stepped away.

"You'd better wipe off the lipstick. Red isn't your color."

"It is if you're wearing it," he said, rubbing his hand across his lips. Grinning, he prowled away, attracting the attention of a group of young women. They waved at him, and he paused to speak to them.

She turned away, yet glanced over her shoulder. One woman ran her hand down Ryan's chest, fluttered her eyelashes at him. Ryan laughed, kissed her hand and walked away with a wave. The women stared after him, their gazes hungry and behavior flirtatious.

Julia blinked, her throat tight. She wove between the chairs and tables, a smile fixed on her face. Even though Ryan had done nothing wrong, it was difficult watching women throw themselves at him.

Once Neil and Jeff arrived back in Auckland, Ryan's days were full of rehearsals and most of his nights were spent at the club. He and the rest of the band did the odd set during quiet times to try out their new material and polish up some of the old stuff. They also did rock covers hoping to throw customers off the scent. Everyone said *French Letters* never did covers while on stage, sticking to their own original material instead.

Day by day, night by night Ryan noticed the way Julia distanced herself. If he had a spare moment, Julia practically ran out of the room to undertake a task that required immediate action.

In the early hours of Thursday morning, he and Julia shared a cab back to her apartment.

"We need to talk," he said when they entered.

"Can it wait until after I shower?" Julia avoided his gaze.

"I need to shower too. We'll share."

Julia glanced at him then, alarm smoothing away almost instantly. "I'm tired."

"I don't intend to jump you." This came out sharper than he'd intended, and he grasped for his wavering control. His cell phone rang. "You go ahead while I take this call." He glanced at the screen and grimaced. "Seymour, do you know what time it is?"

"Morning, where I am," Seymour said in his crisp American accent. "Caleb said the material for the new album is coming along well."

"Yes." Caleb hadn't told him their manager had contacted him.

"I've booked you three additional shows in Australia. Another in Melbourne and two in Sydney."

"You could have checked with us first." He didn't want to leave Julia for months again.

"You've never worried about bookings before." Seymour sounded surprised.

No time like the present to drop the truth into the conversation. "I'm married, Seymour. I have a wife to consider." He stopped talking, waiting for an explosion.

"Fuck. Are you crazy?" Seymour's voice rose with each successive word.

"I don't believe so." The shower shut off. "I can't discuss this now. You can shout at me in Wellington. I presume you're coming down for the concerts."

"I am now," Seymour said crisply. "Does anyone else know?"

"Caleb, Jeff and Neil and a few of my wife's friends."

"Keep it that way." The phone slammed down before Ryan could tell Seymour what he thought of his order.

Shaking his head, he went to take his shower. Julia was

already in bed when he entered the bedroom. He crawled into bed with a sigh.

"Bad news?"

"Seymour has booked us three more shows in Australia."

"Oh." She paused. "I'm sure your fans will be excited."

"You're not and that concerns me more. I don't want to leave you."

Julia reached over and switched off the bedside lamp, plunging the room into darkness. "It doesn't matter."

Irritation swept through Ryan, and he fumbled with the lamp on his side of the bed. He blinked at the flare of light. "I'm leaving to meet work commitments. I have every intention of coming back to you."

He caught a trace of doubt in her expression, and his temper swirled higher.

"I don't understand why you won't believe me. I've done nothing to harm our marriage. I don't drink, do drugs. I've never been unfaithful to you. I'm not your ex."

She bit her lip, unwilling to look at him once again.

"If anyone has a reason to be pissed and full of doubts, it's me. I can't remember, but I'm sure I would've bought you an engagement ring. You don't wear it." His pointed gaze focused on her left hand. "And a wedding band?"

"I haven't noticed you wearing your wedding band," she retorted.

Ryan frowned. "I have one?"

"You said you intended to wear it on a chain around your neck. I can't see one either there or on your finger."

"I had a ring?"

"A gold band I had engraved before you left on tour."

"I didn't find a ring with my stuff after I was discharged from hospital."

Her brows rose, the touch of challenge increasing his indignation.

"Check with Caleb. He collected my gear for me. He'll tell you there was no ring."

Like a popped balloon, some of the attitude burst from her. "Do you think the muggers stole it?"

"Doesn't that make sense? They took my phone and wallet and left me for dead. They must've taken my ring. My watch too," he added. "Caleb said I used to wear one my parents gave me."

Julia closed her eyes. "My ring is in my jewelry box over there on the dressing table. I wore it on a chain around my neck until I—" She broke off with an audible swallow.

"Until you what?"

"Never mind." Moisture welled in her eyes, and she blinked rapidly to clear it. The stubborn jut of her chin told him she didn't intend to enlighten him further, yet swift on the heels of determination came a flicker surprisingly similar to guilt.

Ryan climbed out of bed and strode over to the jewelry box. He lifted the lid off and scanned the contents. The pair of rings on a gold chain was underneath a pendant necklace. He plucked them out and returned to the bed. "I want you to wear them, and tomorrow we'll go to a jeweler's and buy a new wedding band for me."

Her eyes widened as if he'd surprised her. "You'd do that?"

"Of course. I want people to realize I'm married. I want no one else except you." He took her left hand and slid on her wedding band. She didn't protest. She said nothing, merely stared at her hand. He slipped the sapphire and diamond engagement ring on her finger before reaching to tilt her face to his. "I love you, Julia, and I want everyone to know it."

CHAPTER TEN

Julia studied the sparkling rings on her left hand. Even though she'd worn them for four weeks now and Ryan had left to do the *French Letter* tour dates, the rings never failed to pull her up short. She was married to Ryan Callander, and he was wearing a wedding band too.

"Julia, are you listening?" Susan demanded with the air of one who'd asked several times already.

Maggie chortled, her eyes sparkling with a warning that she intended to tease. "She's daydreaming about Ryan and what they're going to do together when she flies over to Sydney for the weekend."

"Have you noticed Dubois, the lead singer of *French Letters* is wearing a wedding ring?" Christina asked.

"Funny you should mention that," Susan said, and Julia couldn't fail to see the faint quiver of lips when her friend attempted to pull off serious. "I noticed *French Letters* are playing some of the original songs Ryan and Caleb have been performing on stage at *Maxwell's*."

"I noticed too," Maggie said. "I wonder if we should call in the lawyers and sue. Start a social media campaign, a call to action. I mean, it's shocking the lengths some artists will go to to obtain new material." She didn't even try to restrain her amusement.

"Have you been keeping secrets from us, Julia?" Susan asked. "A husband is a pretty big secret. Somehow I think we've only scratched the surface of this big, fat juicy mystery."

"We should do a fan dance," Julia said. "You know—the big feathery fans."

"Oh no," Christina said, shaking her finger back and forth. The tinkle of her bracelets highlighted her refusal to allow a change of subject. "We should do the dance, although I'm not about to take my clothes off no matter how big the feathery fans are to hide my naked bits. We're still talking about your sexy husband."

"Please confirm," Maggie said. "You are married to one of the sexiest men to strut across a stage."

"We've been rubbing shoulders with rock royalty," Susan added. "And you didn't tell us."

Her three friends advanced on her, shoulder-to-shoulder in their demand for the facts.

"Okay. *Okay.*" Julia sighed. "True."

"And the man is wearing your ring," Susan said. "The

same wedding ring that has the gossip mags abuzz."

She sighed again. "Yes."

"Oh my God. Oh my God. You're married to Dubois!" Maggie shrieked.

"Shush." Julia glanced over her shoulder, relieved to see none of the others had arrived for dance practice yet.

"Julia and Dubois sitting in a tree," Susan sang. "K. I. S. S. I. N. G."

A laugh burst from Julia. "I can neither deny nor confirm that one."

Christina's eyes gleamed behind her glasses. "But you are meeting Ryan for a sexy rendezvous in Sydney."

"Yes," Julia said.

Susan clicked her fingers. "I knew it."

"So what about the fan dance?" Julia asked.

"I want their autographs," Maggie said. "A fan dance would be fantastic. Go for a sort of Gypsy Lee Rose theme. Have you done it before?"

Julia shook her head and grinned. "I'm sure Ryan or Caleb will arrange their friends to sign a T-shirt or something for you. From memory, Mum did the fan dance a few years ago. I can ask her to help choreograph the dance if she's up to it. Janet said she's becoming antsy with all the inactivity while she waits for the surgery, so it might keep her out of trouble."

"I'd be a starter for the fan dance," Susan said. "I didn't realize I'd enjoy dancing so much. It's helped me lose weight and tone my muscles. I could do the strip part as long as the audience doesn't see my boobs."

Another laugh escaped Julia. "Great. We'll do it." Voices trickled in from the front of the club and several young women bounded inside, already wearing their dancing gear.

"Maggie, can you cue the music for us?" Julia clapped her hands together. "Everyone ready? I have two new routines for us to learn. I'd like to do one of the new ones next week if we can get it down today."

The dance practice went well with the dancers from the local dance school picking the moves up without difficulty.

"Great job everyone! I'll see you later tonight." Julia grabbed a towel and dabbed the perspiration off her forehead and upper chest.

"Are you packed?" Maggie asked.

"Not yet," Julia said. "I thought I'd chuck a few things in my bag tomorrow morning. I don't need much for the weekend. I'd better catch up on the bookwork before I go."

"No, Julia, come shopping with us now," Christina said. "I've found a new designer and she has some beautiful dresses in stock. They'll pack well."

"I'll do the bookwork for you," Susan said. "It's no problem."

"Ryan won't ring until later tonight," Maggie said.

"All right," Julia said. "We've worked hard recently. Let's do it."

The following afternoon, Julia boarded The Air New Zealand flight to Sydney. She caught a cab to their hotel in Darling Harbor and checked in. A big bunch of pink roses greeted her when she walked into the suite, the floral bouquet filling the room. She set down her bag with a thrill of pleasure heating her through.

A small square parcel sat on the end of the bed, wrapped with a pink bow. Julia opened the card and smiled, a tingle of anticipation widening her grin until her lips ached. She shook the box, breathless with anticipation when she pulled off the lid. The scent of rich chocolate rose to greet her. The box contained several handmade truffles plus three small jars of some sort of chocolate substance and a selection of brushes. A saucy laugh spilled free. Edible body paint.

"Fun gift," she murmured.

A key card sounded in the door, and she turned.

"Julia?" Ryan's overnight bag thumped to the floor.

"Ryan!" She flew toward him, leaping into his arms from a few feet away. Her legs wrapped around his hips as she clung to him. He laughed, twirling her around. Then he was kissing her, wrapping his arms around her as if he hadn't seen her for months. Julia opened her mouth to him, slid her hands down his back, touching as much of him as she could manage.

"God, Julia," he said. "I've missed you so much."

She kissed the tip of his nose. "Don't you like sharing a

room with Caleb?"

Ryan snorted. "The dude snores."

"I missed you too. So much. How long do we have?"

"The rest of the afternoon. I need to be at the stadium by seven."

"And after the concert?"

"I'm all yours," he said. "I told Seymour I didn't intend to stay for long tonight. Caleb and the others are taking care of the parties and promo stuff."

"In that case," Julia said, releasing her tight hold of him. She gripped the hem of his black T-shirt and drew it over his head, feasting her gaze on acres of masculine flesh. Next, she yanked on his belt and unfastened his jeans, her frantic hurry making him laugh.

"Boots first, sweetheart." He sat on the edge of the bed.

Julia knelt by his feet and pulled off his boots and socks. Soon he was naked and she stood back to admire her husband. His gaze rested on her, his easy smile absent for once. Each rapid breath showed in the rise and fall of his chest while his feet were spread apart, arms resting at his sides. His cock jutted out, jerking a fraction under her scrutiny.

"Are you going to do more than stare?" Gritty arousal filled his voice.

"Definitely, but we do have the entire afternoon."

"On the bed," he snapped out, urgency glittering in his pale blue eyes.

Julia chuckled but kicked off her shoes, hastening her pace. "Let's have a quickie before we get to the good stuff."

He cast a considering glance down at her bare legs, his gaze an invisible caress. "Very thoughtful of you to wear a skirt. Much quicker."

"And here I thought you favored skirts because they showed off my legs."

"Very true. Condom?" He was suddenly all business, yet his gaze slid to her breasts and lower, the visual touches leaving a trail of acute expectation. Her hands trembled as she reached into the side pocket of her pink handbag.

When she glanced up, condom in hand, he was closer than she'd expected. Her lips formed an O, but the corresponding sound didn't have time to escape because his mouth slammed over hers, drinking in her startled cry. Then all she could do was feel—the press of his hard body as he backed her against the nearest wall, the chill of the unforgiving surface at her rear, and the heat of his mouth as he ravaged hers. She gripped his shoulders to enjoy the ride.

His right hand was a warm weight at her hip, the nip of teeth a bolt of pleasure-pain at her neck. That hand slipped under her skirt and inched up her leg. Tiny pinpricks of delight followed his questing fingers. When he lifted his head his lips were red, slightly swollen. Sexy. One-handed, he tugged the buttons of her silk shirt. One flew off making a sharp *ping* against a coffee table. He lowered his head, taking hard bites out of the swell of her breast. She gasped, holding his head to her, wanting, craving more.

Somehow he loosened her bra, and then his lips surrounded her nipple, sucking strongly. An echoing pull twanged between her legs.

"Ryan," she whispered, trembling under his relentless attention.

The hand under her skirt continued exploring until she squirmed, every particle of her body consumed with desperate hunger.

"Need your fingers on me," she said on a plea.

He licked around her nipple and ran his fingers over the thin lace of her panties. Back and forth. Back and forth. His fingers slid underneath, curled then he gave a hard yank. Fabric ripped and he peeled the lace away from her body.

"On the bed," he said.

"Oh, this is a comfortable quickie."

"Damn straight." He dragged her away from the wall and half threw her onto the mattress. "Where did you put that condom?"

She unfurled her left hand to display the condom while remaining sprawled on the bed, her skirt hiked up around her hips.

Ryan grabbed the foil packet and ripped it open. Then he was on her, pushing into her, filling her while his mouth feasted on one breast. A wild symphony of sensations slapped her around, making her catch her breath and hold onto him for dear life. The scent of him, fresh and citrusy, familiar, made her nostrils flare. And the heat. The heat seared her flesh and pulled her into a place where pleasure ruled. It roared across her mind, tweaked at her breasts and streaked down her legs, growing bigger. Better.

Her fingers dug into Ryan's shoulders, her hips lifting into each of his rapid thrusts as she savored the hard and aggressive act, the curl of heat. A ball of liquid pleasure roiled in her loins, and her belly clenched. He nipped the side of her neck, the burst of pain detonating something inside her. She flew apart, only held together by her contact with him. He powered into her again, a decisive stroke then he stilled, fully embedded, a loud groan squeezing past his clenched teeth.

"Damn, Julia. I love you so much."

They stayed connected, Ryan buried in her until the need to breathe drove her to struggle from beneath his larger bulk.

"Are you going to tell me you love me one day?"

Her gaze shot to his before uneasiness made her eyes slither away. She used to tell him all the time. Before.

"I—" She broke off, swallowed hard. She needed to say something before the pause grew too long.

"It's all right. I get it," he whispered, dropping a light kiss on her lips. "You'll say it when you're ready. For now it's enough to know you're here with me."

Relief struck her at his words, and even more when he didn't sulk in the same way as others in her past. They spent the rest of the afternoon in their room, testing out the luxurious shower before making love again. There was chocolate involved, necessitating another shower.

"Do you want to go for a walk around Darling Harbor? Grab something to eat before I meet the others to leave for the stadium?"

Her stomach let out a rumble, and he laughed.

"I guess that's a yes," she said.

"You could always come with me."

She shook her head. "No. I'll wait for you in our room. How about if I order a special room service dinner for us? What time will you get back here?"

"Around midnight. I'll have to make an appearance to say hi to some of the sponsors and reporters, but I promise to make it quick."

"Deal," she said.

RYAN HEARD THE ROAR as he left their dressing room. The opening act was doing a fantastic job warming up the crowd.

"Dubois!"

Ryan turned at the name. Seymour, their manager jogged to catch up with him.

"I definitely need you to attend the after-concert function. I promised the press some sound bites from you all."

"Remember, I said I can only stay for half an hour." Ryan held up a hand when Seymour opened his mouth to protest. "No, my wife is in town for the night. I want to spend time with her."

Seymour scowled.

"I've done everything you asked me to do," Ryan said. "But I am not about to ignore the fact I have a wife, a woman I love."

"What if she talks to the press?"

"She won't." He didn't hesitate in his reply. Julia wasn't vindictive. Caleb, Neil and Jeff trotted out of the dressing room in full makeup, faces painted in white and blue, their true identities safe from exposure.

"Ready to rock and roll?" Seymour asked in a hearty voice.

"Walk in the park," Neil said, waggling his drumsticks at their manager.

They waited in the wings, and when their cue sounded, they ran onstage.

"Dubois! Dubois! Raine! I love you, Beauchamp. St. Clair, look this way!"

Fans of both sexes chanted their stage names. Ryan and the rest of the band waved back and took their places.

"One, two, three," Neil said, his low voice the prompt

for their first song. A few beats later Ryan kicked in with the lyrics and a roar of approval rippled through the arena. Ryan flashed a grin at Caleb, not far from him. Doing something he loved, being loved—life didn't get better.

Still sweaty from their performance, Ryan followed Caleb into the room Seymour had set aside for the press. As they walked to the front of the room and took their seats, the clamor ceased and the press members snapped to attention. Most of the journalists peered intently, as if they wanted to see beneath the blue and white makeup each of the band still wore.

Seymour remained standing. "You'll have half an hour for questions."

"And make it snappy," Jeff said, winking at the nearest female reporter. "I have a hot date tonight."

A chuckle swept through the room.

"All right," Seymour said. "We'll take your questions one by one. Yes, sir, you in the front."

"This question is for Dubois," the man said. "Is it true you have a two-year-old son here in Sydney?"

The room burst into chaos, the questions coming fast, one after another. Ryan stared at the middle-aged journalist until Caleb dug him in the ribs.

"I have no idea what you're talking about." But the reporter did, and his steady expression told Ryan he believed his source. A club of trepidation beat Ryan over the head, silent protests rioting through him as he took in the man's certainty. Pain shot through his temples and he lifted one hand to surreptitiously rub it away. *Crap. His makeup.* He placed his hand on his thigh instead. "I don't have any children."

"But it's possible," the man said.

Ryan shrugged, pretending confidence while his stomach squeezed to a painfully tight knot. No way. He'd always been so careful. Fuck, Julia would kill him, if she didn't shove him out of the apartment first. "No comment."

"Next question please," Seymour said, his quick glower at Ryan promising discussions in his future.

"Your lover had plenty of comments when I interviewed her," the journalist said.

"Next question please," Seymour repeated.

"Do you make love in your stage makeup?" someone shouted.

"Doesn't someone want to ask an original question?" Caleb demanded. "It'll make your story stand out from the others." His grin remained pasted in place, but Ryan had little difficulty in discerning the underlying snark.

Ryan maintained his comfortable sprawl, only half listening to his friends answering questions. A kid. *No way!* He'd know if he had a child. Surely the woman would have contacted him? Hell, maybe not. Julia was his wife and she hadn't caught up with him during their

European tour. The journalist captured Ryan's gaze, his
eyes narrowing and a hint of excitement coloring his
cheeks. They stared at each other for a long moment
until Ryan broke contact when someone called his name.
Luckily Neil took the question because Ryan only heard
white noise.

"We're working on a new album," Neil said. "It's some
of our best work yet."

The reporters blinked at the piece of information and
two asked questions about their progress.

"You're wearing a wedding ring," one of the female
journalists piped up during a brief lull, her nosy gaze
fixated on Ryan's wedding band.

"That's because I'm married," Ryan said, barely
restraining from scratching his cheek. The last thing he
needed was smeared makeup.

"When did you get married?"

"Who is she?"

"Does your wife see you without makeup?"

Ryan had told Julia the press would ask questions. "I've
been married for almost a year. No, you don't get to know
her name, and yes." He winked at the female reporter. "My
wife gets to see me without my stage makeup."

"What will your wife say about your love child?" the
initial reporter shouted.

Ryan didn't want to consider her reaction because
it scared him. While they'd worked things out, their

relationship was still fragile. He tapped his index finger against his thigh, weighing his response before deciding it was best to stick to the tried and true. "I have no comment."

A few minutes later, Ryan signaled Seymour and indicated he intended to leave. In the dressing-room he showered, rid himself of his makeup and changed to jeans and a scruffy T-shirt. Black boots and a cap advertising his favorite rugby team completed his dress. With well-practiced sneakiness, he exited the dressing room and left via a rear door. Meeting no one's gaze, he merged with the crowd still loitering outside the stadium. He'd have trouble getting a cab, but the rail station wasn't far from the arena. He'd be back in Darling Harbor in no time.

When he entered their hotel suite, Julia was doing stretches and working on a new routine for the club.

"Hi." She unfurled her body until she stood at full height and threw herself at him. "How did the concert go?"

"Brilliant," he said, then scowled, the remnants of the tension headache nipping at him. *A son.* Nah, it was a bullshit story aimed to cause chaos with his marriage. "The press conference afterward not so good."

"Oh?"

"Later. It's not important, just the normal crap. How's the new routine going?"

"Not too bad," Julia said. "I figured I might as well do something useful since there was nothing on the telly."

"Do you still want room service?"

"All sorted," she assured him, glancing at the clock in the small kitchen area of the suite. "Our meal will arrive in half an hour. I'd better shower before it arrives."

"Don't get dressed," he said, his gaze skimming along the lines of her body and lingering on the tight tank top and leggings. "I'm only going to rip your clothes."

Julia snorted. "You owe me some lingerie."

"I'll take you shopping tomorrow morning. It will be my pleasure." Ryan enjoyed watching her as she sashayed away to the bathroom, happiness pushing away the anxiety about the reporter's revelations. Super sexy and all his. He couldn't lose her.

Yeah, the kid was another one of those nuisance pieces, full of rumors and pretense rather than fact. Some woman who wanted her minute of fame in the press, and he'd provided the vehicle for her to propel herself into the spotlight. Still, he'd better tell Julia about the latest over their dinner. Plus the fact Seymour had booked them one more concert—a small intimate thing to celebrate someone's birthday. The girl's parents were paying megabucks, and he and the rest of the band were donating the proceeds to charity. As much as he wanted to beg off this concert, he couldn't.

The shower went on and Ryan stalked to the phone. He

had no idea what Julia had ordered for dinner, but a bottle of champagne wouldn't go astray.

A tap on the door announced the arrival of their meal. Ryan opened the door and let the room service waiter wheel in their dinner.

The waiter set a table for them, complete with candles and a pink rose in a vase. Ice clinked as he arranged the champagne in an ice bucket. "Would you like me to open it for you, sir?"

"Please," Ryan said.

With the champagne taken care of, Ryan tipped the man.

"Thanks. Will there be anything else?"

"Not tonight," Ryan said.

With a final nod, the waiter left, closing the door behind him.

Julia wandered from the steamy bathroom, dressed in a fluffy white robe. He walked to her and pulled her against his chest, breathing deeply at the warm skin of her neck. She smelled of flowers.

"I missed you."

She pulled away, lacing her fingers with his. "You have to do your concerts. Besides, we're together now. Let's eat. I'm starving."

Ryan followed her to the table, pulled out a chair and seated her. "Champagne, madam?"

"Please." Her eyes twinkled, and in that moment he fell

in love all over again.

"Would it work for you if we kept the length of tours shorter, if I was away for a month at the most, instead of six months?"

"You'd do that for me?"

Ryan squeezed her shoulder and plucked the bottle from the ice bucket. "You're my wife, Julia. Your needs are important."

"Yes," she said with a bright smile that echoed in her eyes. "That would work. But I get it. I understand you have to tour to promote your music. It's part of the job."

He handed her a glass and poured champagne for himself. "To us."

She grinned and clinked her glass against his. "To marriage and love."

"To my beautiful wife." Emotion swelled inside him then, something bright and precious. Knowing she was willing to make their marriage work, and she was mentioning love meant everything to him. It gave him hope for the future, for the time when they'd start a family and grow old together.

Julia's stomach let out a demanding grumble. "Told you I was hungry."

The tomato soup flavored with the bite of herbs disappeared rapidly. Ryan dunked up the remains of his soup with a piece of bread. "Beats a diet of pizza and burgers. What else do we have?"

"Smoked salmon fillets and salad with coffee and truffles for dessert. What happened at the press conference? You seem distracted," she added, her gaze skewering him—a demand to tell her now.

Ryan pushed away his bowl, no longer hungry. He sighed, not wanting to break the spell when things were going so well between them. "A woman has come forward and is telling everyone I'm the father of her baby."

Her sharp inhalation broke the silence. "And are you?"

The even tone hurt way more than a shout or cutting words of anger. "I haven't slept with another woman since I met you."

"That's not what I asked."

"No." He shrugged, unhappily admitting the truth to himself. "I don't know." Before Julia he'd slept with other women. Too many women. The kid's age made it possible and that sent uneasiness rioting through him, as did the reporter's attitude. "I don't have any details, but I suppose there's always an outside possibility."

"I see." Once again the even tone.

"Damn it. I never pretended to be a saint before I met you. Caleb and I both partied hard, but the minute I met you everything changed. This kid—it's probably not even mine. If she takes things further, a DNA test will provide the truth."

Julia nodded slowly, her chest rising and falling as she heaved a sigh. "You're right. No point worrying until we learn the details. I wasn't a saint before I met you either, so I don't have the right to call you on things that happened before we met."

Ryan bit back a scowl, not liking what she was saying. Double standards. True, but he couldn't help the way his mind worked. He fiddled with his soup spoon, unwilling to look at her or let her witness any of his misplaced jealousy.

Julia reached across the table, placing her hand on his. "Thank you for telling me. It can't have been easy."

"No. I...I... God, I don't want to lose you again."

"You won't. I'm here to stay." Although the words were encouraging, the lack of ease in her smile alarmed him.

Julia woke from a fitful sleep. Ryan was curled around her, skin pressed to skin and they lay as close as two people could. He'd told her the truth, kept to their deal about honesty even though he'd risked alienating her with the news.

She wasn't that brave.

She swallowed, remaining motionless in case she woke Ryan while her mind continued to chase around a mental obstacle course. She'd lied by omission. Tonight had been another opportunity to tell him about their baby—the one she'd lost. It would've been the perfect time to tell her husband that because of the fallout from the STD, it was unlikely she'd conceive again, not without difficulty. Tears welled and flowed down her cheeks, soaking the sheets, yet she remained still, biting her bottom lip to stop from sobbing. Guilt filled her, mired her down and refused to let her move forward.

Ryan loved kids. He'd want them some day. She owed him the truth.

She must have fallen asleep at some stage because she woke hours later when Ryan tugged back the curtains. His phone rang, and she heard him murmuring to someone.

"I don't believe it."

Julia rolled over. "What? What is it?"

"The woman has served legal papers on Seymour. I need to take care of this."

"Now?"

"I'm sorry, sweetheart. What time is your flight?"

"Midday." Julia thought rapidly. "You'll be back in Auckland after the extra concert next Saturday, right?"

"Yeah." He sat on the bed beside her, his expression tight and worried. "I don't want to go."

"I don't want you to leave either, but the sooner this is done, the sooner we can move on. You go and see Seymour, and I'll get myself to the airport." She paused and swallowed before looking him straight in the eye. "We'll get through this, Ryan." Although upset, she manfully held her stuff together and was glad she did.

His smile was a bright thing of beauty. It stole her breath and made her anxious at the same time. The little voice at the back of her mind told her, *now!* She should tell him now.

She couldn't.

She didn't.

Instead she returned his smile, let him kiss her goodbye, burying the truth deep down inside and pretending waiting to hear news of a child—Ryan's child—didn't matter.

CHAPTER ELEVEN

BACK IN AUCKLAND, THE week dragged. Julia spoke with Ryan on the phone each morning and most nights too. They chatted about the club, about his music and the tour and skirted the topic sitting like a dinosaur between them. Heck, there was no point discussing it until Ryan heard the results of the DNA test.

Her phone rang. "Julia, have you seen the paper this morning?" Maggie asked.

Something in her friend's tone sent a frisson of warning darting through her in a pinball fashion.

Ryan. The baby. It was bad news.

"No, I never have time to read the papers."

"Where are you?" The urgency in her friend's voice confirmed her fears.

Julia squeezed her eyes shut. "I'm at the club. I wanted to run through the routine for the fan dance on the stage again. Susan will be here any minute."

"Wait there for me," Maggie said. "Connor and I are on our way."

Julia hung up, forcing her mind away from Ryan and their problems. Someone knocked on the front door, and she went to answer it. Susan rushed inside, her cheeks blooming with health. She was looking good these days.

"I'm so psyched about this dance. I thought I'd be petrified, but it's such a tease. I can't wait to do it the first time in public."

Julia nodded, forcing her mind into a reboot. *Focus.* "Me too. I hope the crowd will enjoy our new routine."

"They will. We're getting good numbers through the door each night. The bank overdraft has disappeared."

"Maggie and Connor are on their way," Julia said. "You ready to rehearse your number?"

"Yep." Near the stage Susan tossed off her coat to reveal her leggings and tight T-shirt beneath. She vaulted onto the stage, grabbed her white feather fans from the dressing room and returned. Julia started the music and watched Susan go through her moves.

"A bit slower at the start," she suggested. "Make each move subtle and languorous. Speak with your hands and your eyes to the audience. Yes! Perfect." When the music came to a crashing crescendo and faded, Julia clapped. "You will wow them tonight."

Someone hammered on the front door, and Julia's

phone rang. Maggie, she saw when she glanced at the screen. "That's Maggie and Connor. I'll let them in."

One look at their concerned faces, and she realized it was bad. She stood aside and wordlessly gestured for them to enter. After shutting and locking the door behind them, she turned to them again. "It's Ryan's kid."

"Yes. Wait, you knew?"

"Ryan and I talked about it last Saturday. How old is the kid?" She held her breath, not sure she wanted to hear the answer. Ryan had remembered the woman and said her story sounded legitimate. The worry in his voice had amped up her own fears. Now the truth thumped her like a death blow.

"They say he's almost three," Connor said.

Julia's shoulders slumped while she groped for mental control. Okay. Everyone had things in their past—mistakes—that came back to haunt them. Lots of people had illegitimate kids, and they dealt with the problem. Ryan had said the woman was probably after money. Ryan had enough not to miss giving some away. "Is there anything else?"

"No, just speculation about Ryan's identity."

"Is the woman's name mentioned?"

"She's referred to as Leah K," Maggie said. "I doubt it's her real name."

"Okay." Julia walked past them and grabbed her fans off the stage. Not the time to think about this now. She *had* to hold herself together until she was alone. "Since you're here, you can critique my routine. Music please, Susan."

Julia spoke crisply, not giving her friends a chance to comment or speculate further. Fiercely concentrating on the here and now, the things in her control, she sucked in a deep breath while waiting for the opening notes. The sultry tones of the popular old song from the thirties rang through the club, and she flowed into her routine. She was the lady in the song, seductive and sensual, arms flashing. Teasing. Each flutter of the fans designed to conceal yet reveal, erotic tension at its best. She became one with the music, strutting, kicking her legs while keeping the fans in constant movement. The song came to an end and she stilled her two fans in front of her body, a little out of breath with the exertion of the dance.

For a long moment, not one of her friends made a sound, then the three of them started talking together.

"That was amazing," Maggie said.

"You make me look like an amateur." Susan's breathless opinion.

"Sex with clothes on," Connor added.

"Imagine Julia's act with the right lighting and when she's in costume." Susan went up on stage and gave her a swift hug. "You will wow the crowd tonight."

JULIA KEPT BUSY FOR the rest of the day, and each time her mind wandered to Ryan, she yanked it back to work. She checked the books, did the roster for the following month and cleaned up the dressing room. She rang her mother, who'd come through heart surgery well, and popped out to visit her in the hospital. If she kept moving, her fears wouldn't catch up with her. She wouldn't stare at her phone, waiting and wondering why Ryan hadn't rung her.

One by one the staff arrived. When she walked outside to open the front doors and do her normal stint of meet and greet, she found a line. The cool breeze snatched away her startled laugh.

"Good evening," she said to the group of women standing at the front of the queue. She recognized them from the previous weekend. "Thanks for coming back. Go straight on inside."

"Thanks!" one woman said as she and her friends wobbled through the doors on their skyscraper heels, delicate and musky designer perfumes combining into an original bouquet.

"We love *Maxwell's*," the last of the women said. "It's so classy."

"Thank you."

She greeted the next couple with a smile and nodded to several customers who'd visited the club during the previous week. Repeat customers. They were doing something right.

After half an hour Julia strolled back into the club and watched one of her acts with a critical eye. She nodded when the music ended, unsurprised by the enthusiastic applause. The girl was good. She checked her watch and headed for the changing room.

As usual, it was a cacophony of noise and dancers and color. Comforting and accepting. Julia dropped onto a chair in front of a lighted mirror and added more eye makeup. She pulled her hair out of the upswept do she'd started with and bushed it until the blonde strands glowed under the lights.

"All ready?" Susan asked.

Julia nodded, shrugging aside the unease that had crept inside her while she sat still. "Let's do it and get the crowd warmed up for our special acts tonight."

After her first routine, the evening passed in a flash. She rang Janet and ask how her mother was doing.

"She's doing great," Janet said. "The doctors are pleased with her recovery and say she should be out of hospital sooner than they'd envisaged."

"That's great news! Give her a hug for me, and tell her I'll pop in to see her tomorrow morning."

Julia mingled with customers and soon she was ready to introduce her new act with Susan performing straight afterward.

The onstage lights dimmed. Julia walked silently into

position, despite the spiky heels of her red shoes, despite the faint tremor of her knees. She struck a pose, caught her breath and waited. The spotlight snapped on, enclosing her in a beam of light.

The aliens have got me. The fanciful thought curved her lips, and just like that her nerves settled.

She could do this.

The musical introduction started. Her fans fluttered above her head, showing the audience her sparkling black and red bra top and matching long skirt. The light caught the sequins, her sashaying steps displaying the long length of her legs, encased in fishnet stockings.

The vocalist crooned, his husky voice coming faster as the song swelled around her on the stage. She strutted, swayed, created mesmerizing patterns with each swish of her feather fans, yet never revealing her torso to the audience. Her back arched. She stripped the skirt off with one quick twist of her wrist. The silky fabric sailed toward the wings, one of the other dancers whisking it off the floor.

Julia glanced at the audience, those seated in the front near the stage. They weren't talking. They weren't drinking. They were watching her with avid attention.

The sultry music ebbed and flowed, the singer's voice a husky croon slithering through her veins. The front closure of her bra top opened with a flick of her fingers and her breasts spilled free. She tossed the top into the audience and winked toward the man who caught it. Her feather fans fluttered, teasing. Always moving, yet never revealing her bare breasts.

The singer held the last note of the song before tailing off. Silence fell. Julia bowed, fans concealing her partial nudity. The crowd remained quiet, and the only audible sound was the pounding of her heart.

Frowning, she straightened, peering out at the shadowed club. Hadn't they enjoyed her dance? Had she misjudged her audience? She opened her mouth to ask where she'd gone wrong. Then she noticed her customers standing. The applause and cheering was the sweetest music she'd ever heard.

Ryan stood in the back of *Maxwell's* with Caleb at his side. Awe battled with an edgy side of jealousy as he stared at his wife gliding about the stage. Although the fans screened her body, he realized she was almost naked. Hell, every red-blooded male in the room knew her breasts were bare, their lustful thoughts almost deafening him.

"Your wife has spoiled me for every other woman," Caleb said. "I wish she had a sister."

The roar in Ryan's head was loud and thunderous. It certainly stifled rational thought. His hands balled and his body tensed.

"Don't hit me," Caleb said after a sidelong glance. "Man, you're in enough trouble without adding brawling to the list."

"I don't like these men looking at her," Ryan snapped.

"They can't see nothin'. She hasn't flashed her boobs at anyone."

"I can hear what they're thinking." Ryan's weight shifted from foot to foot, desperate to rid himself of the influx of edginess. It struck him that this was what Julia had tried to tell him when she'd mentioned the single women who hung around *French Letters*.

"A lot of women come on to us," Caleb pointed out. "That must be difficult for Julia."

"Fuck off," Ryan said, irked because Caleb read his mind way too often for his comfort.

"All I'm saying is that this is a job for her. She's turned a sleazy strip club into something classy and sophisticated."

Caleb's reasonable tone pissed him off. His friend was right, and that pissed him off too.

"What are you going to tell her?" Caleb asked.

Caleb wasn't talking about the club or Julia's performance. He meant the kid who was currently sleeping in the apartment he used to share with Caleb before he'd moved in with Julia. They'd left their grandmotherly neighbor babysitting. "The truth." Yep, Caleb was doing his best work on Ryan's last nerve. "What do you expect me to do? I can't hide the kid. He's my son."

Caleb cursed under his breath. "I hope I don't have any rug-rats out there. I never want to go through today again."

"You want to try wearing my shoes," Ryan snapped. Realizing he was delaying seeing his wife, he straightened. "I'm going to talk to Julia."

"Good luck. I'll be propping up the bar, watching the action if you need me."

Up on the stage another performance was ready to start. The crowd seemed to straighten, the heightened interest a living, breathing thing. A purple spotlight flicked on, highlighting a masked brunette woman in a tight purple gown. She held two large purple fans in her hands. The surrounding patrons took a collective breath as they waited for her to commence.

Ryan wove between the tables, eager to see Julia again. A snatched phone call wasn't enough. A security guard stood in front of the door leading to the dressing room. Ryan didn't recognize the man.

"You can't go in there." The man might be elderly, but he possessed the solid hulk of a rugby forward, the crisp white shirt and black trousers all of Julia's frontline staff wore highlighting the fact he'd kept up his fitness. "Staff only."

"I'm Julia's husband," Ryan said. "I'll wait while you check with her." He appreciated the man's caution and didn't mind waiting.

The man returned with Julia on his heels. She bore a wide grin of welcome.

"Ryan, I didn't expect you so early." She threw her arms around him and squeezed him hard.

"Caleb and I were able to catch an earlier flight." Despite the audience, he kissed her, taking his time. *Delaying the talk*, his conscience prompted because his son was a ticking bomb. "Do you have a minute?" He'd promised the babysitter he'd be back as soon as he'd spoken to Julia.

Her smile died, the pleasure at seeing him fading from her expression. "You look serious."

He shrugged. "I need to tell you what happened in Sydney."

Julia led him into the office and shut the door, proud of the way she'd greeted him without a hint of the anger and confusion or the plain panic that roiled like a ship in a storm inside her. "I saw the paper. The kid is yours."

"Yes."

Something in the way he answered made her scrutinize him more closely. She swallowed, afraid of what he might say next. Mentally, she ordered herself to calm down, but fearful thoughts collided with the secrets she'd kept, shoving her frustration levels higher. She cleared her throat, intending to ask about the child. That wasn't what emerged. "I can't have children," she said baldly, cringing inside while she waited for the fallout. "Not easily because of the STD I caught."

"What?"

She closed her eyes, pain stabbing her chest, making it difficult to breathe, to think. She groped for the words to make him understand. She should have told him about the baby weeks ago, but talking about it brought back horrid memories of pain and feeling achingly alone. Loss. Guilt. The panic she'd experienced when she couldn't contact Ryan, the awful moment when she finally accepted they were over. "I've tried to tell you a dozen times."

Ryan gaped at her. "But we talked about children. Why didn't you tell me when I moved in with you?"

"How?" she demanded, her nostrils flaring. Heat flushed her cheeks as she fought the urge to fling an empty coffee cup at his head. "It's hard enough to think about, let alone talk to anyone else. You told me you wanted children when the time was right. What did you want me to say?"

"Do your friends know?"

It was difficult to read him, with his hard face devoid of emotion. Yet his pale blue eyes bored into her, demanding answers, returning her glower with interest. She swallowed hard and studied her red shoes, noting the scuff on the left one.

"Julia."

God, she had to tell him. She scowled at the offending scuff mark. "When you were on tour in Europe, I discovered I was pregnant." Her lips twisted as her words tumbled out. "Hell of a shock since I was on the Pill. I tried to contact you and failed."

"Julia." Ryan moved closer and gripped her forearms. "What happened to the baby? Did you—" He broke off, his breathing sounding harsh in the enclosed office.

"I miscarried," she snapped, lifting her chin to meet his unfounded accusation. She would never...he could shove his thoughts right back where they came from. "I didn't abort the baby or give it away. I miscarried, Ryan. Christina and Susan found me unconscious in my apartment." She couldn't see, couldn't focus on him, and realized her face was damp. She sniffed, knuckling away the moisture from her eyes. "I didn't understand how much I wanted the baby until they told me I'd lost it. When the doctor told me it would be difficult to have more children I was devastated."

"Hell!" He dragged his hand through his dark hair, leaving it ruffled. He took half a step toward her and halted, his arms falling to his sides. "I'm sorry. All this happened about the time I was mugged?"

She nodded, unable to speak past the lumpy obstruction growing in her throat. Her hands clenched and unclenched. He had a child. She groped to deal with the thoughts swirling through her mind, the white noise, the pain of losing their baby. Guilt because she kept wondering if she'd done things differently with her pregnancy. A rush of envy and resentment because he had a child with another woman.

"I can't...I...can we talk about this tomorrow?" When

she glanced at him, she caught his look of anguish and it ricocheted back to her, making her feel as if she rode an out-of-control train. Nausea curdled her stomach, and she swallowed.

"Hell." Apparently his go-to word. His fingers worked his hair until the strands stood to attention, as agitated as him.

His reluctance to look at her forced a cry from deep in her chest. It halted at the clog halfway up her throat.

"Fuck." His harsh whisper throbbed with pain. "Julia, I'm sorry. This isn't good timing, but I need to tell you something."

"What?" Something in her gut coiled tight and kept tightening until she wondered if she might snap and fly apart.

"The mother of the kid didn't want him. She signed him over to me."

Her mind whooshed. It buzzed and clanged with frenzied thoughts, with helplessness, with stabs of pain.

A child.

She gasped for air. The reality of Ryan's son forced raw memories to the surface—memories of her baby, their baby. The stunned surprise on learning she was pregnant. Her initial panic, slowly replaced by the joy that encroached, one day at a time. She'd wanted to be a mother, wanted it so desperately. Then came the sheer black terror of knowing there was a problem, the agonizing cramps in her belly, the knowledge she was losing her baby. She pressed her right hand to muffle her cry of pain, the memories she'd concealed and boxed away ripping jagged holes in her composure. "I...I...can't. I..."

Ryan stared at her, his lips pressed together, his impatience obvious in his glance toward the door. "I have to go. I'm staying at my old apartment tonight with Caleb and need to get back to relieve the babysitter."

Julia stared at him, unable to pluck the requisite words from her cement-mixer mind. The pause lengthened. Heck, she didn't know what she should say or think when grief was jabbing her with pointy spears, bringing back the nightmare in glorious color. Blood. Pain. Concerned faces. Doctors. Pure, blinding white agony and dark days filled with nothingness.

"Right," Ryan said in a hard voice. "I'll meet you for breakfast in the morning. We have decisions to make." His body tense, he hesitated a fraction longer, but when she remained silent, he stalked from the office, closing the door quietly behind him.

The tiny snick sounded like gunfire, as if he were closing the door on their marriage.

Julia stumbled to the closest chair, turmoil crashing her senses, nausea still heavy in her belly as she squeezed her eyes shut. She pressed a hand to her chest and concentrated on small, even breaths when what she really wanted to do was crawl under the desk and hide.

A tap sounded on the door seconds later. It opened and Maggie popped her head through the gap. "Connor and I are—what's wrong?" She hurried to Julia. Connor followed, pausing to close the door behind him.

Julia blinked and, after groping for words to explain, started talking, sparing a thought for the irony. She managed to talk to her friends—the Tight Five—but not to her husband. "I told Ryan about the baby I lost. Blurted it out when he told me about his son. I couldn't...I couldn't... The mother doesn't want her child."

"He's keeping the kid?" Maggie sounded surprised.

"I don't...I think so." She threw up her hands in disgust at herself. "All the pain of losing our baby sort of exploded inside me. I froze, and I...he left."

"Why didn't you tell him about the baby earlier? I presume he was the father?" Connor asked.

Julia gave an irritable shrug, angry at herself as well as Connor for stating the obvious. "I know. I know. I should've told him, but I decided the divorce would go through and it didn't matter. And the longer I left it, well, the harder it seemed to introduce the topic. He told me how much he wanted kids. What was I meant to say to him? You have no idea how guilty I am for losing our baby. I keep thinking I could've done something differently. If I'd realized I was pregnant straightaway and stopped drinking."

"Don't be stupid," Connor said. "I was there when the

doctor told you it wasn't your fault and sometimes there's no medical reason for a woman to suffer a miscarriage."

"Just because the doctor said it doesn't mean my mind accepts his word."

"What are you going to do? Where's Ryan now?" Maggie asked.

"He's gone back to his old apartment. We're meeting for breakfast."

Connor crouched in front of Julia. "What do you want to do? There is another angle to this. You don't need to be a biological parent to make a good mother or father. You've met my stepfather. He loves me, and he has been a damn sight better parent than my real father. Talk to Ryan. Tell him what you're feeling. Maybe this is a chance to start afresh."

"But he's away on tour all the time, and I have the club to run. Neither of us knows anything about children. Our work schedules don't fit with children."

"Julia, you're just making excuses," Connor informed her bluntly. "Talk to him, tell him everything. Lots of parents work at demanding jobs and still have great kids."

Maggie sent him a silencing look and grasped one of Julia's hands. She squeezed it tightly. "No one ever said it would be easy, but you can make it work—if you want. Do you love Ryan?"

Julia gave a jerky nod, not having to consider her answer.

"Then it's simple. Don't wait until the morning,"

Maggie said. "Talk to him now. Listen to what he says and ask questions. We'll drop you off at his apartment if you want, but don't leave this until the morning. It will be that much harder if you stew all night."

The stupid lump in her throat kept growing and wouldn't disperse, no matter how many times she swallowed. She croaked, "Okay."

"Promise?" Connor persisted.

Julia gave a tiny nod. "I'll do it."

"I'll tell Susan you're leaving. She'll take care of the club." Connor turned to his wife. "Meet you both out front."

Half an hour later, Julia stood at the door of Ryan's inner-city apartment.

"Don't make me come and buzz the apartment for you, Julia," Maggie said, her tone faintly threatening.

Julia flipped her friend off and squared her shoulders. She pressed the buzzer. Only then did she hear Connor drive off. They'd been right to wait. Her friends knew she was behaving like an idiot, and the temptation to run might prove appealing. She'd promised Connor she'd tell Ryan everything, even her fears that he'd no longer want her now that he'd learned the truth.

"Yeah."

She identified the tinny voice as Caleb's. "It's Julia."

When she reached their apartment and tapped on the door, it flew open. Caleb glowered at her.

"About time," he snapped.

"Can I come inside?"

In one of the rooms to their right, she heard a child crying. "Is Ryan in there?"

Caleb's mouth was tight with anger. "Kid's crying for his mother. Heartless bitch."

Julia followed the heart-wrenching sobs and found herself in a small bedroom, only big enough for a single bed. Her gaze darted straight to the child who sat in the middle of the narrow bed. His inky black hair was tousled, curls sticking out on one side of his head while the rest of his hair plastered to his scalp. Tears rolled down his red cheeks, his cries tearing at her. He was little and obviously confused.

Ryan stood by the bed and glanced up when she entered. Frustration and fatigue lined his face.

"Ryan," she whispered.

"Julia." His tone was cool, his expression cautious.

"How long has he been crying?"

"Ever since we arrived home from the club," Caleb said from the doorway.

"Why don't you get us a drink of some description?" she said to Ryan. "I'll see if I can settle him."

Ryan hesitated.

"Go," she said, turning her attention to the boy. He stared at her with big, blue eyes. Ryan's eyes. Her mouth rounded in surprise. The boy was a miniature of Ryan, and so obviously his son. The hair. The pale blue eyes fringed by dark lashes. The same shaped face. "What's your name, sweetheart?"

He took a noisy breath and stared at her. Finally he gnawed on his bottom lip. Julia could see he was trying to work out who she was.

"I'm married to your daddy," she said, her heart twisting at the tears swimming in those blue eyes. "What is your name?"

"Alex." He sounded scared, and anger at the mystery mother swelled inside her.

"Are you tired?" A rhetorical question because his thumb had crept into his mouth. "Why don't you lie down, and I'll pull the covers over you."

"I want Eddie." His bottom lip trembled as he looked around the room.

Suddenly the clues made sense. She scanned the room, her gaze alighting on two bags. In one, she found a battered teddy bear. She held it up. "Is this Eddie?"

Alex nodded, reaching for the soft toy. He settled back, the bear clutched in his arms. His thumb drifted back to his mouth and his eyes fluttered shut. Julia backed from the room, leaving the door ajar so they'd hear him if he woke again.

Caleb and Ryan were in the lounge, both holding a beer and speaking in low voices. They stopped on seeing her, faces blanking. She'd been the topic of conversation.

"Is he asleep?" Ryan asked.

"He was crying because he didn't have his soft toy."

"Hell, I never thought of something like that. He didn't say. Was there a toy with his stuff?"

"A teddy bear."

"Thanks. I poured you a glass of wine," Ryan said, gesturing at the glass on the wooden coffee table.

Caleb stood. "I'll leave the two of you alone."

Julia took a sip of the white wine. It was crisp and tart and delicious. She wandered over to the window and made out the brick wall of the building next door before taking a deep breath and turning to face Ryan. "Alex takes after you."

His expression turned rueful, but when he focused on her, there was an edge of caution, as if he worried about her reaction. "It was like jumping back in time and looking at my reflection."

"What happened in Sydney?"

He puffed out a breath of air and rose from the leather couch. "I received word of the DNA test results. My lawyer rang with them. As soon as it was official, Alex's mother delivered him to my lawyer like a damn parcel." He sucked in a quick breath, anger echoing in his voice. "Her lawyer drew up a legal document, and she signed away her parental rights. Evidently, her fiancé doesn't want to raise another man's baby."

"She gave him away." Julia struggled to understand a

woman who rejected her child because he was an untidy interruption in her life. Adoption at birth—sure—but Leah K had kept Alex until it suited her, then disposed of her son, casually tossing him away in exchange for the man and the perfect life she sought.

"Yeah." Ryan sighed again and nailed her with a determined look. "I'm keeping him, raising him as my son. He's an innocent kid. None of this is his fault, and he shouldn't suffer for it."

Julia nodded, agreeing with him even as familiar anguish brought a rush of moisture to her eyes.

"Will you stay the night?"

"I..." Thoughts tore through her mind, tangling and tripping over each other. This was too much to take in right now. "No. I need to get back to the club and I want to check on Mum."

"You're running away."

The words, stark and true, drew her up, sparked her temper. "What do you expect? You've thrust your son on me without warning, and I feel as if I've had my feet ripped out from under me. I need time, to work things out in my own way."

Ryan stared at Julia, aware of the fear rushing into him. From the moment he'd seen Alex in the lawyer's office he'd known he couldn't walk away. Yeah, he'd suspected Julia would be upset, but he'd decided once she saw Alex and heard the details he'd talk her around.

Fuck, how the hell was he meant to realize Julia was dealing with all this other stuff, still grieving for the loss of their child?

Emotions shifted inside him, blindsiding him with their rawness. His hand tightened around his beer bottle while he struggled to find solutions, to battle the pissed sensation he experienced every time he recalled Julia's confession. *Damn it!* Giving up Alex wasn't an option, but he couldn't lose Julia over this either.

He glanced at her pale face, took in the tense lines of her body. Part of him wanted to draw her into his arms and offer comfort, but her expression screeched *back off*. Hell, maybe she was right. They both needed time because the other part of him wanted to rip into her, to tell her he'd had a right to know about the miscarriage. It had been his child. His loss too. The familiar twangs at his temples signaled an oncoming headache.

"How long do you need to think?" Agreeing to her suggestion was a bad idea. Time apart was what started this cluster fuck.

She met his gaze this time, and the grief in her eyes almost buckled his knees. They needed to get past the hurt. *Honesty.* Yeah, they both needed a good dose of candor.

"I'm worried if I back off and give you too much time, you'll decide divorce is the only option for us." His words shimmered in the air between them—a softly spoken gauntlet. "The one thing I am certain of in all this bloody mess is that I've never stopped loving you. I want you in my life."

Some of the tension left her shoulders, and she angled her body toward him. "I didn't realize marriage was so hard."

A bark of laughter escaped him. "Ditto on that, sweetheart." Their shared grin, brief as it was, released some of the pressure in the lounge.

"Just a few days," Julia said. "I promise I won't run away or do anything stupid." This time Julia's manner was easier, and when he closed the distance between them, she didn't remind him of a wild animal, intent on escape.

He took her wine glass and set it and his bottle aside. "A few days, but we talk every day."

"I promise."

Relieved she'd conceded that much, he tugged her into his arms, ignoring the sharp darts of his headache. She relaxed against him and some of his dread dispersed. Something about this woman called to him. Even when his memory had let him down, he'd known she was there, waiting for him. After all that, he didn't intend to walk away and lose her, but he wouldn't reject his son either. Alex was the innocent in the middle of the mess, and he had to do right by him.

CHAPTER TWELVE

"JULIA, VISITORS!" THE JERK of Susan's head indicated the entrance of the club.

Julia clicked off the music and her dancers came to an abrupt halt. The newest one at the end of the row gave a sigh of relief and bolted for a water bottle.

"Sorry to interrupt," Ryan said.

Julia grabbed a towel. "Take five," she said to her dancers and wandered over to join Ryan and Caleb. Alex clung to Ryan's hand, trying to hide behind his legs.

Ryan leaned in to kiss her cheek. "I rang Mum this morning to tell her about Alex. She wants to see him, so I've decided to take him down for a visit."

She'd wanted time, she reminded herself, biting back her instinctive protest. "For how long?"

"A week. Maybe longer," Ryan said.

She gulped at the *maybe longer*, and he must have seen

some of her anxiety.

"Our deal still counts. We talk via phone instead of face-to-face. What's the best time to ring you?"

"Around ten in the morning. Around ten at night would work too."

"Okay. I'll talk to you tonight," Ryan said.

She should say something, but her brain had turned sluggish. Instead she stared at him, one of those stupid blocks in her throat. Caleb made a sound, a sort of growl, and Ryan shifted his weight, his expression hardening.

"Mum is expecting us for lunch, so we'd better head out."

Julia nodded. Ryan gave her a quick kiss on the lips, and they were gone.

"The kid looks like Ryan," Susan said.

"Alex. Yeah, he does." She clapped her hands for them to resume, shoving aside her fears she'd made a huge mistake in letting Ryan leave. "Let's get back to work on the new routine."

The next morning Julia sat at the breakfast counter, nursing a mug of coffee. Her apartment echoed with emptiness, despite the background music and the cheerful prattle of the breakfast radio jock. She'd gone to bed early for her— around three in the morning—and tossed and turned, finally falling asleep cuddling the pillow Ryan had used. His scent had both comforted her and made her aware of his absence, of how her request for time and space loomed like a mistake.

What if he decided not to come back? What if he gave up on them?

The two questions twisted together in the small hours of the morning, tangling into a multitude of scenarios, none of them ending well.

The phone rang. A glance at her watch told her it was ten, and her heart raced.

"Hello."

"Hi, Julia," Susan said. "I have a question."

Julia hunched her shoulders and lowered her head.

"Julia?"

"Hit me with your question," she said, forcing herself to focus.

"Since the *Farmer Seeks a Wife* competition is coming up and I'm fed up with working at Barker and Johnson, I might hand in my notice. Could I work at *Maxwell's* on a more permanent basis?"

"Of course you can," Julia said, not even needing to think about it. A no-brainer since Susan was a natural. "I need help with the office work too. I'd be a fool to turn you down."

"Really?"

"Yes, really. You can work for me for as long as you want. You'll need time off during the contest, but I knew that already."

"Thanks. What are you doing this morning? Christina

and I are going to do some quick window shopping along Queen Street. We're both looking for an outfit to wear to the initial interviews. Do you want to come?"

"I'd love to. Do you want to meet here?"

"See you in half an hour," Susan said.

Julia raced into the bathroom and jumped into the shower. The cool water and citrus shower gel gave her a lift, and once dressed in jeans and a casual blouse, she functioned with more alertness. She glanced at her silent cell phone, hesitating before dropping it into her handbag. Ryan hadn't rung.

There's nothing to stop you ringing him. She reached for her phone and hit speed dial.

"Julia, I was just about to ring you," Ryan said.

"Great minds think alike." *Stupid. Tell him you miss him.* "How's Alex?"

"He's still quiet and withdrawn, but he's taken to my parents. He's in the kitchen helping my mother do some baking."

"That's good."

"I told my parents about you."

"You did?"

"I figured I'd get it out all at once. A wife. A kid." Humor laced his voice this time, his husky tones curling through her.

She found herself smiling. "How did they take it?"

"Pretty well. I told them the mugging had made me

lose some of my memories. They already knew that because they've had to remind me about a few things. Luckily, there aren't as many gaps now." He paused then whispered. "I got off lightly with my parents' reaction considering. They want to meet you."

"Did you tell them about the club?"

"Yes. I said that's why you couldn't make the trip with us."

The doorbell buzzed. "Hold on a sec, Ryan. Christina and Susan have arrived. I'll just let them in." She buzzed in her friends and waved them toward the coffeepot before continuing with her phone conversation.

"Mum wants us to stay for longer. She said it will be good for Alex."

"But you are coming back?"

"Of course we are." His voice softened into the intimate tone he used when they were alone late at night. "I miss you."

"I miss you too."

"We're going to the beach this afternoon."

"Have fun."

"Talk to you later, sweetheart."

He hung up before she could reply, but just hearing his voice eased some of her fears. He'd sounded glad to hear from her.

"Ready to go?" Christina asked, her bracelets doing a musical tinkle when she picked up her brown handbag.

"All set," Julia said. "Ryan told his parents about me."

"They didn't know?" Susan asked.

"We'd intended to tell them and perhaps go down for a visit together, but Alex happened." Julia signaled a passing cab, and they piled inside.

"Queen Street, Downtown, please." Christina sank back against the leather seats of the luxury taxi. "I guess you both had a lot to sort out first."

"Yes." If Ryan had told his parents about their marriage, he intended to stick around. He wasn't playing games. No, that wasn't fair. Ryan had never played her, which was why she'd liked him so much. His straightforward manner was the reason she'd agreed to marry him—that and her feelings for him. The distrust had come from her side.

Something to consider.

The cab slowed for a red light, and Julia glimpsed a poster advertising a women's magazine. A photo of the members of *French Letters* decorated the cover. She turned away, not wanting to read the headline. "What did you have in mind for your outfits?"

"Something classy, yet not too sophisticated that it scares off our farmer," Christina said. "We don't want him to think we'd refuse to get our hands dirty."

"Sexy without being too blatant. A fabric that won't crease too much," Susan added. "The last thing we need is to get off the bus looking as if we've slept in our clothes. And we want to divert his mind to sexy possibilities, not decide we're a sure thing."

Julia rubbed her hands together, forcing glee. "I'm looking forward to this."

"An outfit that says feminine yet capable," Christina said.

"A mission," Julia said.

"We needed the full team on this one," Susan said. "Maggie is meeting us there."

Julia thought about all the things she needed to do at the club before pushing them to the back of her mind. "You have my full attention, at least until four. I want to pop in and see Mum."

Maggie was waiting for them at the Downtown shopping center. She cocked her head, listened to their list of requirements and her lips quirked a fraction. "This sounds like serious shopping. Just as well I wore my comfortable shoes."

Gradually, they made their way up Queen Street, stopping whenever a shop window snagged their attention or Christina's insider knowledge told them the stock in a shop might work for them.

"This reminds me of the makeover you gave me," Maggie said while they waited for Christina to try on a pale blue dress.

"So much has changed since then," Susan said. "I handed in my notice at Barker and Johnson this morning and told them I wasn't coming back after my holiday."

"Good for you," Maggie said. "Connor has decided to look for something more challenging too."

Christina emerged from the dressing room to survey her reflection in the full-length mirror. "It fits well, but it's not quite the image I was going for. It's too sweet."

"What about this one?" the shop assistant asked, selecting a ruby-colored dress off the rack.

"Yes." Christina gave an approving nod. "But not for me. Susan, this has your name written all over it."

"But it's red," Susan said. "Isn't it a bit eye-grabbing?"

"Go." Maggie made shooing motions toward the dressing room.

Julia's phone beeped, showing an incoming text. Photos. She scrolled through the attached photos of Ryan and Alex at the beach. Her heart twisted when she reached one of both of them together. Ryan bore a grin while Alex was more pensive, the beginnings of a smile lifting the corners of his lips.

"Ryan took Alex to the beach." She handed her phone to Maggie to show her the photos.

"They look alike," Maggie said.

After showing the shot to Christina and Susan, Julia took a last look before putting her phone away, smoothing her thumb across Ryan's face. The apartment echoed without his presence.

Susan emerged from the dressing room.

"That's the one," Maggie said.

"It's perfect," Julia said.

"You look stunning," Christina agreed. "The color works on you."

"That was easy," Susan said, sounding surprised. "It just goes to show you need to try the clothes on before rejecting them."

"Where to next?" Julia asked. "The department store at the top of the street?"

"They have a sale on some of their designer labels," Christina said.

Maggie flashed a grin. "Let's move on out then. I might splash out on some lingerie and give Connor a surprise."

"La, la, la," Susan said while handing over her credit card to pay for the dress.

"Perhaps you should buy lingerie too, Julia," Maggie said, her grin widening. "Ryan might appreciate it."

Susan sent them a disgruntled glance, sharing it around before snapping the clip on her handbag shut. "I'm going to buy lingerie too."

"Smart," Julia said, winking at Maggie. "Always be prepared."

They wandered past several shops, chattering and teasing Susan about lingerie. At the main doors to the department store, Julia glanced at one of the display windows and came to an abrupt halt. Maggie plowed into her back.

"What's the problem—oh," Maggie said.

The window display was full of children's games and toys, bringing to mind the tiny gray rabbit she'd purchased for her baby. She'd ended up throwing it in the trash and regretted it ever since because the rabbit had represented hope and joy. Her gaze wandered the display to settle on a plush toy owl. It was mainly light brown and had big black eyes. Exquisite chocolate brown felt feathers covered its back. Her mind jumped to Alex and turned to Maggie.

"I'm going to buy a few things. You start looking at lingerie."

"Are you sure?" Maggie seemed to look inside her, attempting to ferret out insecurities and crazy thoughts. For once Julia had none. She knew exactly what she wanted.

"I'm sure."

Alone, Julia took the escalator to the children's department. She paused at the clothes, her attention snared by a miniature T-shirt bearing a popular cartoon character. She chose one in navy blue. In the toy section, she picked up an owl, three storybooks she recalled from childhood and a box of building blocks. While waiting at the counter to pay, she stroked her forefinger over the owl's rounded head and pressed her lips together to keep from beaming. She hoped Alex would like the toy.

Later that night, after arriving home from the club, Julia wandered through her apartment, turning on lights as she moved. In the spare bedroom she found one of

Ryan's T-shirts. She picked it up and pressed the fabric to her nose. His scent only reinforced her loneliness. A reminder of the solitary times after Ryan left to go on tour. Repeating the situation and the isolation... Her throat moved in a hard swallow. No, this was different. Ryan hadn't left her. This was temporary—a break of her doing because she'd let fear get the better of her.

Her cell phone let out its musical summons, and she raced to answer it. "Ryan?"

"Julia." His warm voice brought a rush of pleasure.

"I got the photos. Is Alex settling down? Is he talking to you?"

Ryan laughed, a low intimate sound that made her wish they were in the same room. "A little. It's Mum he follows around like a baby duck."

"I took time off and went shopping with the girls today."

"Good for you. Did you buy something sexy?"

"I might have." Julia slipped into flirtation. "That's for you to find out."

"Now that's something to look forward to."

A shiver worked through her, a fluttery, delicious sensation and something she'd mull over later. "Are you working on songs? Or rehearsing?"

"No, this is pure holiday for us. We'll start rehearsals again once we get back to Auckland. I talked it over with Caleb. We're going to stay for two weeks."

Two weeks. Julia gripped her phone until her forearm

hurt. She released the pressure and bit her lip to stop herself from blurting out her objections.

"I was looking through the papers the lawyer gave me relating to Alex. His birthday is in just over a week, and we've decided to have a party for him. Give him a chance to meet his cousins and look forward to something."

"How old will he be?"

"Three."

"He'll love a party."

"You could always come down."

Julia sighed. "I'd love to, but I can't leave the club, and I want to keep an eye on Mum."

Excuses, her conscience taunted her.

"When will she come out of the hospital?"

"Any day now," Julia said, a yawn escaping and slurring her words.

"You must be tired. I'll let you go to bed. Dream of me, sweetheart." The phone clicked, disconnecting the call before she could reply.

"They're letting me out for good behavior. Next week." Her mother's first words on seeing Julia stride into her hospital room.

Julia dropped onto the seat beside her mother's bed. "That's great. Do you need me to come and pick you up?" Although her mother moved slowly, she looked so much better after the heart surgery. "You have roses in your cheeks again."

"That's what Janet said. Janet will pick me up. I will stay with her. It will be quieter and I won't have to tackle stairs. How's that young man of yours getting on? Have the newspapers stopped printing stories about him?"

"I try not to read them. I miss him."

"Of course you do," her mother said. "How is he getting on with the child?"

"Good." Julia pulled out her phone and showed off the photos Ryan had sent her.

"I didn't realize he looked so much like Ryan. You told me he did, but I thought you might have exaggerated."

Julia frowned, accepting the phone back. "Why would I do that?"

"I'm not blind, Julia. You're here and Ryan and Alex are in Tauranga. If you'd really wanted to go with them, you would have found a way, which leads me to believe the pair of you had a disagreement."

"Quite the detective." Julia didn't bother hiding the bite in her reply. Her mother knew her well.

"It's only natural the appearance of a child—another woman's child—would upset a relationship."

"I lost a baby after Ryan and I married. This..." She waved her hand when her mother started to speak. "Alex's appearance in our lives rattled me, and I'm afraid I panicked a little."

Elise's forehead crinkled. "A baby. Oh, hon. You should have told me."

"I was a mess. I told no one the details, not until recently."

"But you and Ryan are still talking?"

"Every day. Sometimes more often. He sends me texts and photos."

"Communication is an important thing in any marriage. Your father and I never talked. That should have clued me in," her mother said ruefully.

"You never talk about him."

"Maybe it's time I did," her mother said. "I've watched you with Ryan. That boy has feelings for you. You care for him too, otherwise you wouldn't be so cut up about your current separation."

"I miss him, and I want to get to know Alex."

Her mother's eyes sliced through her. "You're worried about rejection, about Ryan leaving you."

"My father didn't exactly hang around, and he's never wanted to see me."

"Some men are arseholes." Her mother was blunt, her attitude uncompromising. "We were both better off without him. He was a rich kid, playing at slumming it. When his family learned about my background, they did everything they could to split us up. Francis never put up a fight. All he wanted was wealth and the good times that came with plenty of money."

"But you told him about me?"

"Of course I did."

"And he still didn't want me." The rejection hurt, even though it occurred before she was born.

"No, but I wanted you."

Julia reached for her mother's hand and squeezed, tears welling in her eyes. "Sometimes I forget how much you gave up to keep me."

"I'm proud of you, Julia, and everything you've achieved."

"But I've pushed you away."

"You came when I needed you. I've always known you love me, even if you don't say it very often."

"Oh, Mum." She turned away to grab tissues from her handbag, one for her and another for her mother.

Her mother gave a shaky laugh and wiped her eyes. "I have a point here. From my observations you love Ryan. Do you want to take after your father and make the worst mistake of your life because you're too afraid to take a step into the unknown?"

CHAPTER THIRTEEN

"IS TRADITION IMPORTANT?" JULIA waited anxiously for Ryan's answer, not sure what she wanted him to say. Heck, she wasn't even sure what she thought about traditions anymore. The talk with her mother had skewed her position on what should happen.

"It depends what the tradition is," Ryan said without hesitation. "I like the tradition of marriage and everything involved in the institution. I like the family traditions we have at Christmas and the summer holidays. But sometimes change is good and making new rituals works better than sticking with the old. Why the question?"

Julia sighed down the phone. "Part of my weird mental processes, and I talked to my mother today about my father. What did you and Alex do today?"

"Ah, changing the subject. One day you'll have to tell me about your father."

"I've never met him," she said. "He came from a wealthy family, and they didn't approve of my mother."

"His loss. My gain."

The sincerity ringing down the phone line made her stomach gooey inside. "Thanks."

"Caleb and I took Alex to Rotorua. We visited Rainbow Springs and fed the trout. We checked out the kiwis in the nocturnal house. Mum packed us a picnic lunch, and during the afternoon we visited Whakarewarewa Thermal village and peered down bubbling mud holes. I took plenty of photos."

"Email me some?"

"I'll do it tomorrow," he promised. "How are things going at *Maxwell's*?"

"Susan has started working full time, at least until she does the reality show thing. She's a natural dancer and has the business side down. Best decision I ever made."

"Seymour wants us to go out on tour."

"Oh?"

"I told him we'd only consider short tours, no longer than three weeks. Caleb backed me up."

"What did Seymour say?"

"He cursed a lot. I don't think he's given up. He'll wait until we've completed the new album and ask again."

A tap sounded at her office door and Susan stuck her head inside. "Carrie has rung in sick. Can you fill in for her?"

"Ryan, I've got to go. I'll talk to you tomorrow."

"I love you, sweetheart."

"Bye," she whispered and hung up, a wide smile curving her lips. They never seemed to run out of things to say to each other, and they'd talked more in the last few days than they'd managed during their early marriage.

She made her way to the dressing room. As usual it was full of chatter and laughing with the women hurriedly removing and replacing costumes.

"Hey, boss," several of the dancers called.

"Ladies," she said, grabbing the roster to take a look. "I might trial the new feather dance routine," she said to Susan.

"How are things going with Alex?" Susan asked.

"Good. Ryan said he's coming out of his shell and interacting more." And she was starting to wish she hadn't told Ryan she needed time. Hearing about their daily adventures left her on the outside. Go figure. She was confusing even herself with her indecision.

"What are you going to do once Ryan returns to Auckland?" Susan asked.

"I'm not sure. Neither of our occupations are child friendly."

"One of my cousins is a nanny," Susan said. "She completed her training the year before last and is looking for a new job. The husband at her current position has wandering hands. Would you like me to set up an interview for you?"

"I'll run it past Ryan." Good grief. Call her stupid but she'd never contemplated a nanny. She whipped off her shirt and wriggled into a glittery purple jacket. "I'll get back to you sometime tomorrow."

"No problem. I told Karen I'd ring her back tomorrow night, so that will work in perfectly."

The more Julia thought about a nanny, the better she liked the idea. It was as if the light bulb moment spurred other thoughts. Positive ones.

"Ryan," Julia said the next day. "Susan's cousin is a nanny, and she needs a new position. Susan asked if we'd be interested in interviewing her."

"That's not a bad idea," Ryan said. "Why don't you talk to her? Why does she want a new job?"

"The husband of her current employer has turned grabby."

"The only one I'm interested in groping is you."

She wished he was there to wander his hands over her right now. "You trust me to make the initial contact?"

"Why wouldn't I? Besides, she's Susan's cousin. That's a sort of a reference there. Susan wouldn't recommend her if she didn't believe she was trustworthy."

Julia could think of at least five reasons why Ryan shouldn't want her to interview a nanny. She hadn't trusted him enough to embrace Alex straight away. No, trust wasn't the right word. Everything happening so quickly had overwhelmed her, leaving her groping to keep her head above water when things were so new between them. Now that they'd talked every day, she was feeling more positive. Ryan didn't intend to give up on her.

"I'll ring you once I've talked to Karen."

"Make sure she realizes she'd need to sign a confidentiality agreement if she takes the job," Ryan said.

KAREN CAME EQUIPPED WITH references and copies of her qualifications. With her long straight brown hair and serious face, she reminded Julia of the Susan she'd met about four years ago at Baker and Johnson. She radiated competence.

"My husband and I both work odd hours, often in the evenings. We have one child, a boy who is almost three." Julia paused to consider her words. They sounded right, and suddenly she wanted to see Ryan and Alex so much a physical ache sprang to life in the middle of her chest. She gasped and realized with a flash of humor that she needed to breathe. "We hadn't considered a nanny until Susan suggested it. What sort of hours are you willing to work?"

"My last position was live-in." Her gaze was level and self-assured and she smiled in a pleasant manner. "I'd want to meet your husband before I agree to take the job."

"Definitely," Julia said, amused yet impressed by the girl's straightforward style. "Ryan would want to meet you anyway. What sort of routine would you suggest for Alex?" She listened to Karen, her confidence, and decided employing her was the perfect solution.

They discussed wages and terms of employment, leaving Julia optimistic when Karen departed. She picked up the phone to call Ryan.

"Hey, sweetheart. How did the interview go?"

"She's perfect. She wants to meet you before she agrees to take the job."

Ryan's chuckle made her grin. "Wants to assess me in case I have wandering hands?"

"I think that's the main purpose."

"You're the only woman I want."

Julia's grin broadened. "I'm pleased to hear it. Karen will be too." The ache of need she'd experienced earlier surfaced again—an intense yearning, now that her thinking was done. Decisions made. "Could I come down for Alex's birthday party?"

"Yes! God, Julia. Yes. When can you come?"

"I need to check with Susan and Christina. Maggie and Connor too. Hopefully, one or all of them will look after the club for me. If they agree I could drive down on the Friday and come back on Sunday afternoon."

"Julia, please make it happen. I can't wait to see you."

The longing in his voice matched the craving in her. "I'll

ring you back in an hour."

"We're off to the beach. Text me instead because I might miss your call."

"Julia's driving down for the weekend," Ryan said, relief jumbling his thoughts and making him want to break into song.

"About time," Caleb said. "I'd almost given up on her."

"I hadn't. She's worth the wait."

"How do you know she's not gonna flip out on you again?"

"We've talked a lot," Ryan said. "About all sorts of things. She doesn't sound as fragile now. My leaving on tour was hard enough, but when she couldn't contact me and lost the baby at the same time—it knocked her. Alex's appearance in our lives was bound to bring back memories."

"But she didn't tell you," Caleb said.

"She was scared. Don't give her a hard time. I love her, Caleb."

His friend gave a clipped nod. "What about Alex? Is she okay with him? If she fucks with his head—"

Ryan understood Caleb's reservations, understood the loyalty that drove his friend to take this stance. "I doubt she'll do that. She should be here later today. Judge for yourself this weekend."

"I intend to," his friend said. "Are we hitting the beach

or what?"

"Alex, are you ready to go to the beach?" Ryan called.

The little boy jumped off his grandmother's lap and bounced up and down. "Swim!"

"Let's go," Caleb said.

"Thanks, man," Ryan said, their quick exchange of glances saying way more.

The beach at the Mount was crowded, but they found an empty patch and set up camp. An umbrella so Alex could play in the shade with the assortment of toys to shift the sand around—a bucket and spade, toy tractors and his favorite grader.

"What a cute little boy," one of the women next to them said. She glanced from Alex to Caleb then to him. "Oh."

"He's my son," Ryan said, manfully biting back his smirk on seeing Caleb's scowl. They'd come across the gay parent thing a few times during the past week.

"Ready for a swim, Alex?" Caleb asked.

"Daddy, swim?" Alex asked, looking at him instead of answering Caleb.

"Sure thing," Ryan said, holding out a hand to his son. The gesture of innocent acceptance when Alex curled tiny fingers around his hand never failed to twist his guts. And now Julia was on her way. Life didn't get much better.

They wandered down the beach, Caleb holding onto Alex's other hand. The Mount was a surf beach, and they entered the water between the flags, paddling in the shallow area patrolled by the lifeguards.

Alex splashed and cackled with glee.

"Here comes the wave," Ryan warned. "Hold tight."

The day seemed to crawl with Ryan checking his watch often. He hoped Caleb hadn't noticed.

"Are you going to stay at your parents' place tonight?"

Oh, yeah. He'd noticed. "I'll ask Mum if she'll babysit for us tonight to give us a few hours of privacy. We'll go out for a drive and walk along the beach."

"Are you gonna get a room?"

Ryan met Caleb's grin with one of his own. "Possibly."

When Alex faded, they headed for home, making one stop at the ice cream shop. A car pulled up in front of his parents' house around ten minutes after four.

Caleb nudged Ryan. "She's here."

Ryan's mother straightened from wiping Alex's face. "About time. You're acting if you have ants in your pants."

"The fictional wife is really here?" his father asked in a gruff voice.

Ryan ignored his friend and his parents to stride outside. His heart raced, and he found himself running, skidding to a stop by the car. Julia opened the driver's door, her mouth wreathed in a wide smile.

He grabbed her, lifting her to wrap her tight within his arms. He nuzzled her neck, breathing in her scent before lifting his head to kiss her. His lips collided with hers, their noses bumped and they laughed. It was perfect once they finally got it right. God, he'd missed her. He hadn't realized until this moment how he'd feared this might never happen, that she'd decide she didn't want to persevere with their marriage. He drank her down, savoring her taste and her lips against his.

"Ahem," his father said.

"I could get the garden hose," Caleb said.

Ryan lifted his head to glare at his friend. "Think about a possible payback."

Laughing, Caleb lifted his hands in a surrender gesture.

"Mum, Dad, this is my wife Julia Maxwell. Julia, my parents Lillian and Patrick Callander." A tremor shook her, and he realized she was nervous. After squeezing her upper arm, he slipped his arm around her waist, aligning himself firmly with his wife.

"Pleased to meet you," she said.

"We'd decided Ryan and Caleb were making you up, but Alex said a lady found his bear. He said she was pretty," Patrick Callander said. "He wasn't exaggerating. Welcome to the family."

"Thanks."

"Who's looking after the club?" Caleb asked.

"They're all pitching in," Julia said. "I owe them."

"Come inside, dear," Lillian said. "I was about to make afternoon tea. Ryan, you can grab Julia's bag."

Ryan picked up Julia's two bags plus a parcel decorated with a red ribbon, struggling until Caleb took possession of one bag. He watched Julia interacting with his parents and smiled a little on seeing Alex trailing behind, his son's attention on Julia.

"That went well," Caleb whispered.

"I had no doubts," Ryan replied. "She'll charm them. You wait and see." He'd finally recalled more about the first time they'd met and how she'd captivated him without even breaking a sweat. Real memories rather than the ones Caleb and Julia had supplied him with when he'd asked. His gaze strayed to her mouth, currently curved in a smile as she handed over the wrapped package to Alex. While everyone commented about Alex's new owl, Ryan calculated how quickly he could get Julia in private, preferably naked.

Later that night, after dinner, Ryan said, "Mum, Julia and I are going for a drive. Would you listen out for Alex? I don't expect him to wake, but just in case."

"If it's privacy you're after, your mother and I are off to the church hall," his father said. "They're hosting a travel evening, and your mother has a hankering for a cruise."

"But we haven't done the dishes yet," his mother said.

"That's what we have kids for," his father said in a cheerful tone. "Do your primping, Lillian. We'll leave in fifteen minutes."

"I'll head home, or Mum will complain she never sees me," Caleb said.

In minutes flat, the kitchen emptied.

Julia's brows rose. "Something I said?"

Ryan took her hand, lacing their fingers together. "The result is that we have a few hours alone. Can't complain about that."

After clearing the kitchen, they went to check on Alex. He was sound asleep, his new owl clutched under one arm.

"He seems a good kid." Julia thought he looked adorable, and she itched to cuddle him or at least stroke the lock of hair off his forehead. She restrained the urge, not wanting to wake him. "I'm glad he liked the owl."

"Mum says he's much better behaved than me."

"Maybe he's frightened he'll get shunted to someone else."

"Not gonna happen." Even if the worst happened between him and Julia, Alex belonged with him.

"I used to have nightmares about my father," Julia said. "Even though I've never met him, it didn't stop me from building images in my mind."

"His loss," Ryan said.

"Exactly, and I'd prefer not to waste words on him. If Karen approves of you and Alex, we should buy a house. My apartment isn't big enough and you share yours with Caleb."

"We can start house hunting as soon as we get back to Auckland." Ryan gripped her hand, not wanting to verbalize his thoughts but knowing he needed to for Alex's sake. "Are you sure? You're not his birth mother. If you have any doubts, tell me now. Later...I don't want you to tell me you're willing to accept Alex and come to regret it later."

His words should have hurt, but she understood. He had the right to question her, and she'd be a hypocrite to object. She squeezed his fingers. Now that she was back with Ryan her heart seemed lighter. She met his gaze. "I'll be honest. It would have been harder if he hadn't taken after you in looks. It would have taken me a little longer to fall in love with him, but those big blue eyes of his. One look and I was toast. Do you know your eyes grabbed my attention first?"

He huffed out a sound that wandered close to humor. "Do you mean to say if I'd had brown eyes you might have picked Caleb instead of me?"

She grinned. "We'll never know for sure." She sobered. "I want you, and I want Alex. Together we'll make a great family."

"I'm glad because we both need you."

Together they wandered back downstairs. Ryan poured her a glass of wine and grabbed a beer for himself before leading her into the lounge. Photos of Ryan and his siblings covered the walls and a grand piano stood in the far corner, signs of a musical family.

"Caleb and I are still determined to keep our tours short. We've talked about it a lot during the last week. We want to focus on song writing. That means I'll be around more. Between the two of us and Karen, Alex will have everything he needs."

He curled a hand around her neck, drawing her closer. Her wine splashed over the edge of the glass, and she set it aside to avoid a spill.

"Alex is great. Once he loses his shyness, he doesn't stop talking. He was quieter tonight, but you wait until he's with his cousins tomorrow at the party." His grin faded. "Tell me about our baby," he said, reaching for her hand.

"I've told you everything."

"Tell me again. Please, Julia. The more we talk about our loss..." He trailed off and gave a helpless shrug. "You understand what I mean."

Their fingers twined together, and she stared at them for an instant. She sucked in a deep breath and shifted her gaze to the vase of apricot roses atop the coffee table. After another inhalation, she started talking. "I discovered I was pregnant several weeks after you left. It was a shock, and I...um...dithered about telling you. We'd never talked about children."

Ryan barked out a laugh. "You never dither."

"I never thought I'd marry. You know about my father. He returned to his wealthy family, wiping us from his mind in the way other people delete computer files." Bitterness coated her words, a twang of pain playing through her—a chord or two of a heartbreaking he-done-me-wrong song.

"You never talked about your parents."

"The man who got my mother pregnant doesn't qualify for the description."

Ryan squeezed her hand in silent commiseration.

"Anyhow, the shock of my pregnancy lasted for a few weeks."

"And when you rang me, you got some idiot woman instead."

"Yeah." She blinked to ease the sting in her eyes.

"What did you do then?"

"I was numb. I walked around in a daze for weeks."

"What about your friends? They would have helped you."

Julia hung her head, unwilling to admit her stupidity. *Tell him everything*. Connor's instruction echoed through her mind. "I didn't tell them. I'm not sure why. Shock." She shrugged helplessly. "I woke up one morning feeling off. I had bad cramps and collapsed in my apartment, hitting my head when I fell. Susan and Christina found me and got me to the hospital."

Ryan turned to her, and she saw the emotion glistening in his eyes. He stared at her, unashamed, as a single tear ran down his cheek. "I'm sorry you had to go through that alone."

Julia ran her free hand over his cheek, brushing the dampness away. "The doctors said sometimes women suffer miscarriages for no obvious reason. I would have lost the baby, no matter what I'd tried to prevent it." The truth of the words hit her—the actual meaning, and she realized she was coming to accept the reality.

It wasn't her fault.

All these months, she'd blamed Ryan. She'd blamed herself. But it wasn't Ryan's fault either. No matter what she'd done, she would have lost her baby.

The acknowledgment seemed to lift a weight off her shoulders. She squeezed Ryan's hand, sending him a misty smile. "I love you, Ryan, and I will do whatever it takes to make our marriage work. I missed you." Her smile turned rueful. "I missed you so much I wore one of your T-shirts to bed every night just to feel closer to you."

"Julia." That was all he said. Just her name before he pushed against her until the distance between them was gone. They breathed together, clung to each other for comfort. "I love you," he whispered against her hair.

They kissed and cuddled, and it was a long time before either of them moved.

"Let's go to bed." Ryan stood and held out his hand to her. It was warm and comforting as his fingers curled around hers.

Side-by-side, they ambled down the passage to his bedroom, pausing to peek at Alex. He was sprawled on his back, one arm clutching his owl. A charming little snore erupted as they watched, and Julia stifled a giggle.

In the darkness of Ryan's bedroom, she stripped off her clothes and climbed into bed. Their naked bodies slid against each other. Their lips met and sweet urgency rose between them. He slipped into her body. Julia cradled him close, arching into him as he loved her tenderly. Her orgasm swelled within her until it became too big to contain, exploding through her in waves of pleasure. When she came back to herself, she smiled, still plastered against Ryan's larger frame.

"Still love me?" he asked.

"Yeah."

"You know you've put me to a lot of trouble," he said, the caress of his fingers down her back counteracting the slight sting of his words.

"But I'm worth it," she fired back.

He sighed, the warmth of his breath feathering across her neck. "Yeah. You are."

"I mightn't have said it much, but I do love you, Ryan."

"Right back at you, sweetheart."

And they set out to prove it all over again.

Curious about what happens to Susan and the reality show? Please turn the page for a glimpse of *Clandestine Lovers*, the next book in my *Friendship Chronicles* series.

EXCERPT — CLANDESTINE LOVERS

DO NOT SCREW UP this speed date. This is your chance to find love. A husband. Everything you want for the future.

"No pressure," Susan Webb whispered as she navigated the gravel path alongside the grapevines and went *off-piste* onto the freshly mown grass. Immediately, the heels of her black-and-red sandals sank halfway to China.

The cameraman following her snickered and kept filming while her arms windmilled wildly to maintain her balance. Thank goodness she'd donned a pair of sexy black briefs this morning. The thought raced through her mind as she teetered on the brink of flashing her bottom to the viewers of *Farmer Wants a Wife* reality show.

"Here, let me help," a husky voice said.

A muscular forearm curved around her waist, the man's

strength holding her upright. A hit of citrus and leather engulfed her while heat massed in her cheeks.

Slowly, Susan turned her head to study her savior. She recognized his chiseled features immediately. Her chosen farmer—Nolan Penrith—and he was even hotter in the flesh. His light brown sun-streaked hair was neatly trimmed but still flirted with the collar of his cream shirt. He wore jeans and a brown leather jacket. Her gaze skirted down past his hips, lingered on the bulge at his groin and moved lower until her stare hit his brown boots. A soft chuckle dragged her attention northward to meet a crooked smile and brown eyes full of amusement.

"Ah, sorry," she said, fervently wishing she could have a do-over. She'd ogled his junk, for goodness sake, right after almost flashing the reality show viewers. Time to fix this situation. She *had* to create the right impression. Her future depended on her actions today. "I'm not usually this clumsy."

"No problem," he said. "Let's get you safely to the meeting spot so we can have a chat."

Susan nodded, embarrassment quashing her ability to format further sentences. Luckily, her mind was still in working order. She grasped one of his arms and attempted to jerk her right foot free, preferably with her sandal still in place so she didn't wobble like an undignified stork.

"That's not the way," he said, a laugh in his voice, and he tugged her back then scooped her up into his arms, striding away and leaving her sandals embedded in the lawn.

Susan became aware of the breeze at her butt and started to struggle. *No, no, no!* This was not happening.

"Don't worry, I won't drop you. A little thing like you doesn't weigh more than a bale of hay."

"That's not what I meant," Susan said, the chill on her backside confirming her fears.

A bark of laughter escaped the cameraman. Susan froze. She was gonna commit murder—if she didn't die of mortification first. She glared over Nolan's shoulder at the man, but all she could see was the blink of light on the side of the camera that indicated everything—including her butt—was being faithfully recorded. *Gah!*

Nolan set her on her feet, and she instantly flicked the back of her red dress down over her panties.

"*Oops.* Sorry about that, darlin'," Nolan said. "Would you like something to drink?" He gestured to a jug of water and another of juice.

Heck, yeah! A margarita would be good about now. "W-water will be f-fine." At least it would be something to do with her hands. Nolan had apologized, so she couldn't hit him. The cameraman, however, was riding a shaky line.

Aware of the camera, she resisted the urge to snap out an insult or roll the cool glass across her cheeks to dispel her embarrassment. Instead, she took a quick sip and fought to regain her equilibrium.

She needed to flirt, needed to speak intelligently, needed to show herself to best advantage.

She needed to excel.

Nolan helped himself to a glass of juice and gestured to the tartan blanket, spread on the ground not far from the table holding the refreshments.

Susan crouched and placed her glass within easy reach, then she gingerly knelt and curled her legs to the side, taking great care not to flash her panties. Again.

Nolan dropped to the blanket with casual ease. "So you're looking for a husband?"

Straight away, her hackles rose and an indignant retort sped to her lips. In her peripheral vision, she noted the cameraman shift positions to get another angle for his shot. She bit back her grumpiness and strove for a witty comeback, something to wow.

"A-are you l-looking for a wife?" *Better, but what was with the stuttering?* She didn't usually stammer. She managed to shape her lips into something resembling a smile. Her friends would see the jagged edges, but it was her best effort when all she could think of was her bottom broadcast on national television.

"It appears so."

The weird inflection in his tone tugged at her curiosity, and she opened her mouth to ask a question.

Before she could speak, he said, "I'm Nolan, which I'm sure you already know, and you, according to my list, are

Susan. Tell me a little about yourself. I believe you work in an office? What do you do in your spare time?"

Oh, heck. Minefield alert.

She hesitated, frantically wondering how to break the news of her career change. "I'm r-really excited to be here, N-Nolan, and it's great to meet you. Um...I...ah...like to dance. I go out with my f-friends to clubs and r-r-rugby matches. Sometimes we go shopping or to m-movies." Her heart hammered like the beat in a fast dance, and she caught her bottom lip between her teeth before releasing it to force her features into a happy, confident mask.

"Not many shops out in the country."

"No, I don't suppose there are." Her fixed smile wobbled and tried to slink away to hide. Was he trying to sabotage her? Had he taken an instant dislike to her?

Too bad.

If they were destined to be together, he needed to know she possessed a steel rod of determination in her spine. She added a touch of sweetness to her smile and hoped she didn't look like a caricature. "The internet works well for shopping. You can buy just about anything online these days from farm equipment to dresses." *Yay! No stuttering this time.*

His brown eyes glazed over and he sipped his orange juice.

Heck, she was losing him.

"Do you enjoy your job?" he asked. "If we hit it off with

each other, would you miss not working?"

"I don't work in an office anymore," Susan blurted.

"Oh?" His dark brows rose to emphasize his surprise. "You gave up your job? You must be very certain of your future."

"No, I have a new job. One of my friends owns a club, and I work for her now."

"What sort of club?"

Susan's heart skipped several beats, leaving her breathless, definitely anxious. "What qualities do you want in a wife?"

"One who answers questions. What sort of club?"

"A burlesque club," she said in a low voice, mortified heat blooming fiery-hot again in her cheeks. She shot a glance at the camera, saw the man zoom in on her face, recording every bit of the unfolding drama.

"You like to dance." It sounded like an accusation.

He was judging her, reading between the lines and making mistakes with his version of the facts.

Susan gave a clipped nod, unhappily aware of the camera. She refused to lie. That was no way to start a relationship. So she was going to crash at the first interview. Didn't matter. She'd done her best, and if she was bowing out of the reality show straight away, she might as well give *Maxwell's* a shout out and gain some exposure.

"I work at *Maxwell's*, a burlesque club on K' Road in Auckland," Susan said. "I take care of the accounts and wages and dance on stage several nights a week."

"You're a stripper," Nolan said, eyes narrowing into disparaging slits.

"You need to educate yourself about burlesque." Susan kept an even tone, refusing to stoop to his level. "Burlesque is not the same as stripping."

"But you do perform on stage."

"Yes, and I'm rather good at it. *Maxwell's* is a very busy place." Nothing less than the truth, and even she heard her shimmering pride.

Nolan stared, and his intense gaze ricocheted through her body, frisking every pleasure point during the journey. A pity he'd set himself up as judge of her morals when he held so much sex appeal.

"I wonder if you'd find the countryside a little quiet," he said. "We don't have shops or movie theatres or clubs."

"I'm open to trying new things," Susan countered. "I've never lived in the country, but I'm sure I'll keep myself amused."

Does Susan catch her farmer?

Grab your copy of Clandestine Lovers
(www.shelleymunro.com/clandestine-lovers) to find out.

About Author

USA Today bestselling author Shelley Munro lives in Auckland, the City of Sails, with her husband and a cheeky Jack Russell/mystery breed dog.

Typical New Zealanders, Shelley and her husband left home for their big OE soon after they married (translation of New Zealand speak - big overseas experience). A twelve-month-long adventure lengthened to six years of roaming the world. Enduring memories include being almost sat on by a mountain gorilla in Rwanda, lazing on white sandy beaches in India, whale watching in Alaska, searching for leprechauns in Ireland, and dealing with ghosts in an English pub.

While travel is still a big attraction, these days Shelley

is most likely found in front of her computer following another love - that of writing stories of contemporary and paranormal romance and adventure. Other interests include watching rugby (strictly for research purposes), cycling, playing croquet and the ukelele, and curling up with an enjoyable book.

Visit Shelley at her Website
www.shelleymunro.com

Join Shelley's Newsletter
www.shelleymunro.com/newsletter

OTHER BOOKS BY SHELLEY

Fancy Free

Protection

Romp

Buzz

Festive

Friendship Chronicles

Secret Lovers

Reunited Lovers

Clandestine Lovers

Part-Time Lovers

Enemy Lovers

Maverick Lovers

Sports Lovers

Military Men

Innocent Next Door

Soldiers with Benefits

Safeguarding Sorrel

Stranded with Ella

Josh's Fake Fiancée

Operation Flower Petal

Protecting the Bride

Milton Keynes UK
Ingram Content Group UK Ltd.
UKHW011954210823
427215UK00004B/310

9 781991 063311